THE CRONE WARS
4

CRONE
UNLEASHED

LYDIA M. HAWKE

**Published by Michem Publishing,
Canada**

CRONE UNLEASHED

August 15, 2023
Copyright © 2023 by Linda Poitevin

Cover design by Deranged Doctor Design
Interior design by AuthorTree

ISBN: 978-1-989457-12-2
MICHEM PUBLISHING

For all of you who are stepping into your power. I see you. I am you. I love you.

In This Series

CHAPTER 1

THE DAMNED CROWS WERE EVERYWHERE.

The woods were black with them. Hundreds sat in the otherwise bare trees that surrounded the clearing, replacing the leaves that had long since fallen from the branches. Others strutted across the frost-tipped grass; more lined the path I was walking and perched along the peak of the house.

But the worst thing?

Unlike the ones that had been my harbingers before, these ones wouldn't shut up.

I stuffed icy fingers deeper into my ears and scowled at the black-feathered horrors as I stomped toward the house They'd been arriving for days, now—the first group had moved into the trees the day after Samhain, and dozens more had taken up residence every time I looked out the window. And with the cacophony they made, I was increasingly annoyed to be the only one who even knew they were there.

Plus, they were giving me a headache.

"The crows again?" Maureen had asked at breakfast as I'd rested an elbow on the table beside my uneaten sausage hash and rubbed a hand over my throbbing temple.

I'd grunted the same non-response I'd been using whenever one of my housemates spoke to me these days, one intended to deter them from sharing their opinions on why the crows were tormenting me, why they didn't think I should go after Lucan, why I should accept my losses after the battle with Morok and just let things be.

Suffice to say that I wasn't much on speaking terms with my fellow Crones right now, and after a moment of pursed-lip silence, Maureen had returned to her conversation with Anne about the day's chores.

1

I'd left the table then and retreated to the woods, too rest-less—and yes, angry—to remain in the house. I'd walked the familiar paths for more than an hour, but I was no better off now than I had been when I'd pushed past Bedivere on my way out the door and forbidden him from following me.

Bedivere, who had his own opinions about the Lucan situation. His own agenda.

On one level, I couldn't fault him for it, because Lucan was, after all, his half-brother. But on another level, as much as I knew I should appreciate how he had taken over Lucan's role as my protector, his constant, brooding stare—along with impatience he made no attempt to hide—had become as wearying as the presence of the crows. And I was done.

I was done with the daily growl of, "Well?" that greeted me when I stepped out of my bedroom in the mornings, behind which lay his unspoken demand to know when I would be going after Lucan. I was done with the former Crones' refusal to help me do so when I'd asked them on Samhain. And I was done with being caught between the two—between Bedivere's insistence that I go, and my housemates' insistence that I stay.

My chin lifted as I stared across the clearing toward the stone house I shared with them all. The shutters sagged, the small windows were coated in grime, and a dead vine clung to the wall beside the front door, giving the building an aban-doned air despite the five humans, one wolf-shifter, and gargoyle that inhabited it. The interior wasn't much better, and there had been no improvements made since—again—Samhain.

Samhain. The night that the veil had thinned, and Edie had crossed over to stand with me and say her goodbyes before she made her final departure from my life. I'd tried to argue, to tell her that I still needed her, but she had only chuckled.

"Need me?" she'd said. *"But you don't, you know. You've outgrown*

me. You've outgrown all of us. And I am so, so proud of you ... how much you've learned about magick and power and yourself. I am honored to have been a part of that journey. But now our paths diverge, because it's time for me to join the ancestors."

She'd hugged me fiercely, then, and her last words to me had been, *"Now go follow that path of yours,"* as she faded from my life forever. In that moment, I had been sure my path led to the Camlann splinter and Lucan, and resolve had filled me even as I'd grieved her loss. But the others ...

The others had all but crushed that resolve.

"Even if we could," Anne had said quietly, *when I'd presented my intention to go after Lucan to them and asked for their help, "we've agreed we shouldn't."*

I'd blinked at her, not quite trusting my ears. *"You've ... you've all discussed this already? Without me?"*

I'd blinked at the others for good measure, and four compassionate but resolved gazes had met mine in turn.

"Our purpose as Crones," Elysabeth had said, *"was always to rid the world of Morok. We did that, Claire, and we cannot chance undoing it. If we were to be successful in opening another portal for you to go after Lucan—and without the Morrigan's powers to aid us, that's a big if—we don't know what would happen. There's no guarantee you'd be able to cross through it, or that you'd end up in the right place, or—"* She'd held up a hand to forestall my response that I didn't care, that I'd take the risk.

"Or," she'd continued, emphasizing the word, *"that Morok wouldn't be waiting on the other side to return."*

She'd been right, of course. They were all right. I knew it, they knew it, and the way Keven carefully kept her back turned on the conversation made me think that she knew it, too. And I didn't blame them for their caution, because if Morok *did* wait on the other side of the portal in Camlann, he would have recovered the half of his powers that had been split from him in that original splinter. The very idea of him returning here with that kind of power made my insides shrink.

Plus, there was the very real concern that the Morrigan herself would take exception to my use of her powers and take them away—along with my life. So yes, all in all, the risks were enormous, and yes, I understood why they refused their help, and yet ...

And yet, the resolve hadn't altogether gone away. It had nagged at me incessantly, peppered my dreams along with images of Lucan's wolf disappearing into the portal with Morok, dogged my every daytime step. It was driving me as mad as the crows were, and now I was done.

"Not if you stand out here all day," my Edie-voice observed dryly. Because the woman herself might be gone, and her ghost might be gone, but apparently I was going to carry on discussions with my version of her voice forever. I rolled my eyes at myself—and the voice—and then sighed. She—it—had a point. Putting the conversation off wouldn't make it any easier.

A movement in the window to the left, the sitting room, caught my eye. I shifted my gaze to the tall, broad-shouldered figure framed there. Bedivere, who hadn't followed me but still watched me. Tension crept up my spine and seized my neck. I shrugged it off in irritation, dug my fingers deeper into my ears, and resumed my march through the crows toward the house.

Done, I reminded myself. Screw the damned harbingers and whatever warning they were trying to impart. I would take my chances with the Morrigan, and with the others. I was going after Lucan with or without them. I had no idea how, yet, but—

The front door to the house opened, interrupting my thoughts. Keven's granite bulk stood in the opening, my traitor of an orange cat draped contentedly around her shoulders, and I squeezed past both into the entry. The gargoyle closed the door behind me, cutting off the crow cacophony outside.

Or at least making it faint enough that I could withdraw my fingers from my ears.

Closing my eyes, I inhaled as I counted to seven, held the breath for another count, and then released it on a third. Then I repeated the sequence. Why a count of seven? I hadn't a clue, apart from having read it somewhere an eon ago. Any other number probably would have worked, too, but the important thing was that it *did* work. My shoulders descended nearer to their rightful place, my jaw unclenched, and my resolve settled deeper into my bones.

I opened my eyes to find both gargoyle and cat watching me, Keven's hand outstretched and waiting to take my cloak. I unclasped the garment and let it slide from my shoulders, then handed it over. She turned to hang it on a hook behind her while I removed my boots and slid my feet into the felt slippers waiting for me.

"Where are the others?" I asked.

"In the sitting room." The gargoyle nodded her head toward the closed door to the left. "There's tea."

"Good," I said. "Because I'm done."

MAUREEN, ANNE, ELYSABETH, AND NIA WERE SEATED ON stools set before the crackling fire, cups of tea balanced on their laps. Nia had one hand extended toward the flames, their long thin fingers spread to absorb the warmth. Elysabeth, perpetually cold ever since the Crones' encounter with Morok in New York City—not to mention her sojourn and near starvation in the fetid cell before that—clutched at a gray woolen shawl wrapped around hunched shoulders. Anne cradled a cup in both hands on her lap, her gray-streaked braid pulled over one shoulder as she stared into the dancing flames and nodded at whatever a highly animated, scarlet-haired Maureen was saying. And beside the window stood the omnipresent dark cloud in the house that was Bedivere.

I hesitated in the doorway. This would be so much easier if I had an actual plan. Any plan. If I could tell them what I needed from them, how I would get to Lucan, how I would get back again. But I had nothing. No plan, no map, no clue as to how I would do this. All I had was the certainty that I had to try—for Lucan, and for myself, because I would never know peace if I didn't.

Maureen's gaze connected with mine across the room, and her hands stopped above her head in mid-illustration of her point. "Claire," she said. She settled her hands back on her lap and exchanged looks with the others, then continued with a note of cheer as forced as any I'd ever heard, "You look half frozen. Come and get warm."

I looked down at the arms I'd wrapped around myself. I was indeed rubbing my hands over them as if chilled, but it had nothing to do with the temperature. At least, not the ambient one.

Avoiding the frost behind Bedivere's scowl, I joined the women around the fire, settled onto a stool, and murmured my thanks as I accepted the cup of tea Nia poured for me. They nodded and set the teapot back onto the hearth at the edge of the fire. Silence sat over us for long seconds, broken by the crackle and snap of a pine log sending sparks up the chimney as I sipped my tea and gathered my arguments. At last, I opened my mouth to speak, but before I could utter a sound, Anne and Bedivere interrupted me in the same breath.

"So," Anne began.

"You're wasting time," Bedivere growled.

The rush of wings filled the room, swallowing both their words.

CHAPTER 2

CROWS EXPLODED FROM THE CHIMNEY AND THROUGH THE room, hundreds of them. They swirled above the heads of the midwitches and wolf-shifter, covered the gargoyle by the door, and then ...

Then they began to caw again.

Still seated—because goddess help me, my reflexes needed major work—I dropped my teacup to shatter on the floor and aimed my fingers toward my ears again. They didn't make it halfway before icy claws grabbed my wrists and held them captive.

Before me, crows coalesced into a long black gown clinging to a woman's figure. A pale, sharp-featured face emerged above the feathers, with a beak-like nose and glittering black eyes that were as cold and emotionless as I remembered them. The hands holding my wrists—those were fingers gripping me, not claws—tightened.

"You," I whispered.

My housemates might no longer have been Crones, but they were still midwitches. Powerful ones. And they were quick to react to the perceived threat in their midst, even if I was the only one who could see it.

In the same heartbeat it took Bedivere to morph into wolf-form, all four women gained their feet, their stools tipping over and teacups smashing to the floor beside mine in shards of porcelain mixed with liquid. With Bedivere's wolf snarling along the perimeter, they formed a circle around me, hands interlocked, chanting words intended to raise protection.

Ignoring them, the Morrigan released her hold and drew herself haughtily tall. She looked down her beaked nose at me

7

—not hard to do, given that I was still seated—and replied, "You waste my gift."

I tried hard not to cringe before her. Yes, she was a goddess, but I possessed half her powers, I reminded myself, and that might not make us equal, but surely—

As if she'd read my thoughts, the Morrigan thrust her pale face so close to mine that I flinched away and only just managed not to fall backwards off the stool to join the spilled tea and porcelain shards. The Morrigan traced a single finger down my cheek to my throat, trailing cold in its wake. A fingernail that was more like a talon pressed into the skin over my carotid.

"You forget that they *are* my powers," she said, confirming my suspicion, "and that I can take them from you whenever I choose."

I swallowed hard against a lump that felt like my heart had lodged in my throat. "I know," I croaked, "and I'm sorry you think I'm wasting them, but Lucan—he—I—" I broke off and tried to gather my scattered thoughts.

At the sound of Lucan's name, the midwitches surrounding me stopped chanting. They stared at me, clearly suspecting that I'd lost it. Bedivere reverted to naked man-form outside their circle; his growl, however, continued. I clenched my hands into fists on my lap and focused on the goddess they couldn't see.

"I can't leave him trapped with Morok," I continued. "He deserves better, and I want to go—no, I *am* going to Camlann to get him."

The goddess that was goddess-ing it over me frowned and withdrew her hand. She stood tall again. "Of course you're going to Camlann. What in all of the Otherworld do you think my birds have been telling you to do for the past fortnight?"

I stared at her. "That I—that you—that—" I flapped my

own hand—at her, at me, at my utter confusion. "Wait. You *want* me to go?"

"Have I not made that clear?"

"Seeing as how I don't speak fluent crow," I snapped, thinking of the time and energy I'd wasted in angst-ing over my decision, "no. No, damn it, you have *not* made it clear."

Ice glittered in the black eyes narrowed on me, and my breath froze somewhere between lungs and throat. I'd gone too far. Spoken too—

"Claire?" Anne asked, her puzzled—and concerned—gaze searching the space within their circle. "Who ...?"

The Morrigan huffed impatiently and threw her arms wide in another flapping of crows' wings as the birds tried to stay in gown form. There was a collective inhale from the others in the room, and then Bedivere and midwitches alike went down on one knee before the figure that had appeared in their midst.

Huh, a part of my brain thought. So that was how you were supposed to behave with a goddess. The rest of my brain shrugged off the idea with an impatience that rivaled the Morrigan's.

Done, it whispered.

I made myself climb to my feet and, with a determined effort, kept my knees from knocking together as they held me upright. I cleared my throat. All gazes in the room turned to me. "I'm going to Camlann," I repeated, just in case the Morrigan had misunderstood me. "To get Lucan."

The Morrigan stared at me for a moment, then looked across the room at Keven, who still stood at the door to the entry and had not, I noticed, knelt with the others.

"You have not told her?" the goddess demanded of the gargoyle.

"I have not," Keven said, her voice flat. Her demeanor lacked any of the respect displayed by the others, and I felt marginally better about my own defiance.

"It is not your place to withhold—" the Morrigan began, but Keven interrupted her with a deep, gravelly snarl.

"You send her to her death!" she snapped. Her hands had curled into fists at her sides, and she crouched as if she might launch herself at the goddess.

Surprise jolted through me, reflected in the others' expressions.

Even Bedivere looked unsettled at the gargoyle's show of temper, his brow furrowed and his gaze darting between her and the Morrigan.

"Keven?" I began, but the Morrigan silenced me with a wave of a crow-clad arm.

Her sharp black eyes narrowed on the gargoyle. "If I do not send her, the world dies."

Keven's fists curled tighter. "You don't know that she'll succeed."

"And you don't know that she won't," the Morrigan said. "*Tell* her."

With her final words ringing through the air, the goddess dissolved into a cloud of black-feathered birds again. They rushed up the same chimney they'd emerged from, oblivious to the flames in the fireplace, leaving the room in shocked silence. The midwitches in a circle around me, Bedivere still naked, Keven looking like she wanted to beat on something, me processing the whole sending me to my death idea …

And my Edie-voice observing, *"Well. That gives a whole new meaning to a murder of crows, doesn't it?"*

THE SILENCE FOLLOWING THE MORRIGAN'S DEPARTURE DIDN'T last long. Keven was the first to move, studiously avoiding my eyes as she turned and lumbered from the room.

The questions from the others came fast and furious, then,

but I dodged them—and the people behind them—on my way to follow the gargoyle.

"Later," I promised. "I'll tell you everything later." Right then, in that moment, I needed answers of my own.

I found Keven in the garden. Despite the encroaching winter and the house's own disinterest in providing for us, she had somehow managed to maintain enough to feed its occupants, and she had stopped now to pluck yellowed leaves from a straggling heal-all. The bunched muscles of the stone back remained turned to me, even though I knew she'd heard my approach.

I stopped behind her. "Tell me," I said.

The gargoyle gave no indication she'd heard. A breeze stirred through the heal-all and encircled my ankles, then swept up my body to slide invisible, icy fingers over my cheek. It carried with it the scent of snow, and I shivered, wishing I'd thought to bring my cloak with me. I reached past a bat-like wing and put a hand on Keven's shoulder.

"Tell me," I said again. Another moment slid by. At last, she turned to face me, and my breath snagged in my throat at the grief written across her features.

She had somehow always managed to show great expression despite the stone from which her features had been carved, but this—this was exceptional even for her. The unutterable sadness that stared back at me from her eyes sliced through my heart like one of her knives through a tomato—minimal resistance followed by a cut that severed it in two.

"Do you remember when Lucan told you that gods and goddesses are fickle at best?" she asked, as if the conversation at the kitchen table that day—our first of many that had changed my very existence—wasn't forever imprinted on my memory.

I nodded.

"I thought she was different," Keven said. "I wanted to believe she cared. I was wrong."

The breath that had caught in my throat turned to shards of glass as I exhaled. I curled my fingers into my palms. I wasn't going to like what was coming, was I?

Keven's voice turned musing as she continued. "I do think her reasons for dividing her powers among the Crones were altruistic enough—at least to begin with. She wanted to stop Morok, and she didn't stay bonded with me, with Morgana, because she didn't want to be corrupted by too much power. But something has changed. Perhaps because she has gone without power—or at least any of note—for too long."

"I'm not sure I follow," I said. "What changed?"

"Fear," Keven said. "She's afraid. If she goes up against Morok herself, she may lose everything. The battle, her power, her very existence." The gargoyle hunched her shoulders, pain carved into her every line. "And so she will risk you instead."

Slivers of glass continued to plague my breathing, and my throat felt raw with imagined lacerations as I swallowed. Hard. Not so much because of what Keven was saying—none of which had really surprised me—but because of how much I suspected she *wasn't* saying. Then, in a flash of insight, I remembered who Keven was. Who she had once been. *What* she had once been—and what that meant.

"Your magick," I whispered. "It's still in Camlann."

The gargoyle stared past me. The breeze had traveled into the nearby woods, its path marked by the lifting and swaying of leafless branches. Crow-less branches, too, because they were also gone, leaving the woods—and me—feeling oddly bereft.

"Morgana's magick resides there still, yes," Keven said finally.

I wrestled with a sense of betrayal. That she could have known this and not told me, that she could have kept such a monumental secret from me ...

"Stay focused," my Edie-voice whispered to me. *"Reasons don't matter right now."*

Perhaps not, I thought acidly, but pursuing them would be a lot easier than facing the consequences it suddenly felt like I was drowning in. I breathed through broken glass again and dug my fingernails into my palms to distract myself from the anger simmering beneath my surface.

"And Morok?" I asked, my voice tight. "Does he know about it?"

"If he doesn't yet, he will," the gargoyle said, and to her credit, she didn't flinch from the words—or the truth. "He will feel its presence in the splinter, and he will search for it. And if —*when*—he finds it, it will give him enough power combined with his own to reopen the portal back here."

Fan-fucking-tastic.

Again, I caught back the words of recrimination because again, Keven's reasons for not telling me didn't matter. Nothing mattered, really. Not when measured against the harsh, bleak reality that the battle I'd fought with Morok had meant nothing. Done nothing. Changed nothing. The dark god was still going to destroy the world and everyone I loved along with it. And he'd start with me.

"What are my chances of stopping him?" I asked. "Truthfully."

"The Morrigan believes that if you find my—Morgana's —magick before he does and take it as your own, it will—it may—make your powers equal to his."

Equal to, not greater than.

Hence Keven's accusation, "*You send her to her death.*"

"Can I defeat him?"

"She hopes so."

"And you?"

Her silence was her answer. I hugged myself against the cold and stared past the gargoyle's shoulder into the winter-bare woods as I digested the many revelations of the past few minutes. The Morrigan had left half her power in me not to keep me alive, but so that I could—she hoped—keep *her* alive. I was to be her proxy.

Or her patsy, if we were being honest, because I was in a race against a god to find a magick that would result in a battle between more-or-less equal powers, and from which it was most likely that no one would be coming back. Not Morok, not Lucan ... and not me.

My breath hitched in my chest, and I tipped my head back and closed my eyes. If I went, I would never see my family again. Never feel the softness of my grandson's cheek against mine. Never sit down to a meal with my fellow Crones and Bedivere. Never work quietly beside Keven in the kitchen or garden. I couldn't even be sure I would see Lucan again, because I had no idea if he was still alive or if Morok—or the goliath—had already killed him. And if I didn't go ...

Fuck, I thought, because if ever there was a case of damned if I did, damned if I didn't, this was it. Stay here and be doomed to die with the rest of the world when Morok returned, or go after him and be doomed to die alone with no guarantee that the rest of the world wouldn't still perish.

"Fucking hell," agreed my Edie-voice.

"I'll need to tell the others," I said to Keven. "Everything."

CHAPTER 3

"MORGANA," ANNE SAID, AFTER WHAT FELT LIKE AN eternity's worth of silence. Her voice held disbelief, shock, and another note that I thought might be denial.

I turned from the window through which I'd been staring without seeing. My gaze flicked over Bedivere, who leaned against the wall nearby, before going to the other Crones sitting on their stools before the fire.

"You're serious," Anne continued. "Keven was—is —Morgana."

"Was," I said, because that was how Keven herself spoke of it. "Yes."

"That's … " Anne trailed off, lifting her shoulders in an I-have-no-idea-how-to-respond kind of way.

"I know." I hugged myself, tucking my hands under my arms. It was drafty here, but I wasn't ready to join the others by the fire. I needed space. Distance. Time to think before we dived into the nitty gritty of how to carry out the Morrigan's death sentence for me. My lips twisted into a sour pucker. Damn the goddess to—

"It's messed up, is what it is," Maureen muttered. "What about the other gargoyles? Were they people, too?"

Reluctantly, I let go of the curse I'd been about to mentally level at the Morrigan, one I probably shouldn't have been thinking in the first place. Maureen's question held an undertone of guilt, and I remembered the general lack of concern or compassion shown by either the Crones or their protectors for the unnamed gargoyles that had served them. I suspected it had been that way for centuries.

I shook my head. "Not that I know of, no. Only Keven."

The group breathed a small, collective sigh of relief, but

15

from the corner of my eye, I saw something else flicker briefly across Bedivere's face. It looked like regret, and a frisson of surprise ran through me. The shifter was so irascible and cold and downright feral at times that I forgot that he, too, was human. Part of him, anyway.

Bedivere's face closed over into its usual scowl.

A small part.

Tiny, perhaps.

My gaze traveled over the faces of the Crones as their discussion of my Keven-revelation continued. Because Crones they would remain in my eyes, regardless of what they called themselves now. Women of great power and wisdom, Keven had said when she'd first told me about us, and with or without their pendants, these women still possessed both those attributes in spades. Attributes I was going to need from them in the coming days.

"—now?"

Anne's last word registered along with the realization that they were all watching me expectantly.

"Sorry," I said, "I missed that."

"What now?" Maureen asked bluntly, in what I was sure was an abbreviated question.

"I ..." I trailed off, because freaking hell, they thought *I* had the answer to that? I'd been counting on them for help. Hoping that one of them would have a glimmer of an idea that would spark something bigger that would lead to a way that—

Out in the hallway, the front door crashed open, and a familiar voice called out, "Hello? Maman? Are you here? I've brought the help you wanted."

I PACED THE KITCHEN FROM ONE END TO THE OTHER AND BACK again, the flagstones hard and cold beneath my feet, as the others—all ten of them now that Natalie and five midwitches had arrived—spoke in murmurs at the table.

Natalie and five midwitches who had arrived because the Morrigan, apparently, had taken it upon herself to request their help. In my name. If that scrawny goddess had been in the room with me when Natalie told me, I was pretty sure I would have strangled her.

I was pretty sure I still would now, because furious didn't begin to describe how I felt. How dared she? How dared she take it upon herself to bring my family back into the fucking disaster she herself had turned my life into? Wasn't it enough that Natalie had almost died once already because of me? I shuddered at the memory of my daughter-in-law's pale form lying unresponsive in the hospital bed, so very nearly lost to her husband and child—my son and grandson—and to me.

I didn't care one iota how quickly she'd taken to witchcraft, or how much she had learned, or how powerful she might be with time and teaching. I would not, could not, let Natalie help.

And my unsinkably cheerful, stubborn daughter-in-law wouldn't take no for an answer.

"But of course I'm helping," she'd said when I'd tried to send her away. *"You're family."*

"Which is why you can't *help,"* I'd retorted for the third time. *"What about Braden and Paul? If something happens to you—"*

"Will I be safe if I don't help?" she countered. *"Will Braden?"*

"I—you—" I'd wanted to lie and tell her yes—oh, goddess, how I'd wanted to lie—but even if I'd been able to, she would have seen through my words. And then she would have ignored them and done as she wished anyway, and—

And *fuck.* I whirled at the door to the garden and stomped back across the kitchen again, fury mingling with impotence mingling with more fury. I had never in my life been so angry.

My hands itched again for the feel of the Morrigan's throat beneath them.

A wall of chest brought me up short. I staggered back a step and looked up into Bedivere's cold gaze beneath one raised eyebrow.

"Are you done?" he asked. "Because this serves no one."

It was on the tip of my tongue to tell him to piss off.

"But he's right," my Edie-voice observed. *"And this isn't just about Natalie, either, you know."*

"And you can piss off, too," I growled at it under my breath. Bedivere's eyes narrowed dangerously. Right. Not as under my breath as I'd intended. I thought about explaining my Edie-voice, decided it would be too much effort, shrugged irritably, and sighed. Then I faced my daughter-in-law for one last beseeching, "Will you *please* go home?"

"No," Natalie replied, crossing her arms for emphasis. "And being angry with me won't change my mind."

"I'm not angry with you," I said. "I could never be angry with you. I'm angry at *her*"—I waved my arm at the ceiling in a gesture meant for the Morrigan—"and I'm angry at this"—another wave, this time with both arms encompassing the world in general as I turned and marched back toward the garden door—"and I'm angry at Morok and the other gods, and I'm angry that we're the ones who have to clean up their mess and—"

I stopped short as gentle arms closed around me—one set, another, another ... a fourth. The Crones. They'd all stood up from the table and come to surround me, to encircle me with themselves, their arms, their compassion. For a moment, I resisted, clinging to my fury, and then I sagged against them as the real reason for my anger surfaced.

"And I'm afraid," I whispered.

"We know, hon," said Maureen, resting her cheek against mine. "We are, too."

CHAPTER 4

I RETURNED TO THE TABLE WITH THE OTHERS AND ACCEPTED the tea that Natalie pressed into my hands, and then ...

Then we stared at one another. Stared at the table. Stared into our cups.

At last, Elysabeth broke the silence. "We'll never be able to open a portal for you," she murmured, resting an elbow on the table and cradling her chin. "Even if we brought in every midwitch in the country, it still wouldn't be enough."

"I know," I said. Opening the first portal had required all of Morok's powers, most of the Crones', and a sizable portion of my own at the time. The Morrigan had since taken the four Crones' powers back, leaving only me. Whatever she expected of me, whatever Bedivere expected, whatever *I* expected, I wasn't anywhere near powerful enough to open another portal, with or without the help of the midwitches.

"But the Morrigan said Claire had to—" Natalie began.

"Then the Morrigan should have told me how!" I snapped. I regretted my tone instantly—as true as the words might be—and sighed as I raked fingers through my hair, tugging impatiently when they tangled there. I shot an apologetic look at my daughter-in-law. "I'm sorry, Natalie. I know you're trying to help, but—" I clamped my lips tight against what wanted to follow, not wanting to hurt her further.

But go home, I wanted to say again. *You belong with your family. I don't want you here. I don't want the responsibility. I can't* ...

Goddess love her, my daughter-in-law came around the table to give me a hug that I didn't deserve. "It's okay, Maman, I know you're under a lot of pressure. That's why the Morrigan brought us here, remember? To help."

Not helping, Natalie. Not helping at all. But even as my lips

19

tightened further and I held back more words that would be just as hurtful as the others I'd swallowed, Natalie released me and planted hands on hips.

"That means there must be another way to get to the splinter," she announced. "We just have to find it."

The other women—Crones and midwitches alike—carefully looked away from her, and from one another. They all understood what the newest witch in their midst did not: that, with all of the knowledge and experience in the room, if no one could come up with so much as a possibility of an idea, it likely meant that none exist—

"Keven," said Natalie. "You know something."

Bedivere grunted in the corner, apparently still struggling with the idea of Keven and Morgana, but I held up a hand against the disagreement he might have voiced. The burly shifter subsided with a grumble, and I stared at the gargoyle by the wood stove. Her back was to the room as she stirred a pot—a pot I knew to contain nothing but potato peelings and carrot tops from the stew that was slow-cooking in the oven. Natalie was right. She knew something, and I'd missed it.

I got up from the table and walked over to join her, putting a hand atop her stone one. "Keven? What are you not telling us?"

The gargoyle let out a gust of air, and a thin ribbon of carrot peel blew out of the pot onto the stovetop. She set the spoon down on the battered wooden counter, then slanted a sideways glance down at me.

"You know that this world is connected to the god world, the Otherworld."

It was a statement rather than a question, but beyond what little she'd told me before—basically, that the Otherworld existed and that was where the gods lived—I had no knowledge of how things worked or were connected. I nodded anyway. I'd catch up on the details later.

Keven grunted as if she'd read my mind, but she continued, "I'm not certain, but it's possible that the Otherworld also connects to the splinters."

I frowned. "But if the splinters have been cut off from our world, how did they connect to the Otherworld?"

"They still exist somewhere," the gargoyle reminded me, "which means they must be tied to something. The Weaver of All—"

"The what now?" I interrupted, because perhaps a few details were in order after all.

"The Weaver," Anne said at my elbow. I hadn't heard her approach, and I jumped at the sound of her voice, almost falling over a broom propped against the counter.

"Indigenous peoples believe—" she broke off and waved a never-mind hand at me as she faced the gargoyle, awe written across her expression. "The Weaver is real?"

"The gods are all *real*, milady, insomuch as humans make them so," Keven said—rather obliquely, I thought, but I didn't want to interrupt again. "The Weaver of All is the origin. The weaver of all worlds and all things, and of the web that connects them."

Anne took a deep breath and exhaled gently, softly. Reverently. She nodded her understanding. "So you think she will have connected the splinters somewhere, too."

"It is what she does."

"So if we can't open a portal," Nia said, "we might be able to travel through the Otherworld to the splinter."

"No," Maureen said, even as Keven's ponderous head shook. "Not us. Claire. She's the only one who still has the power."

The way Keven's gaze avoided mine told me that Maureen was right, but while the others might be surprised by the knowledge, I was not. In fact, I was more relieved than anything, especially because I knew Natalie would stay here, in this world, where she would be safe, and my grandson could keep his mother. I'd never planned to take anyone with me to the splinter in the first place. I'd assumed I would go alone. I'd been certain of it.

I hadn't, however, counted on having to traverse the god world to get there.

I realized Keven was speaking again, and I pulled myself back from the edge of my last thought and made myself focus on her words.

"—human has ever crossed," she said, and I mentally filled in the word *no* that I suspected I'd missed. "The power of a god is needed to open the doorway—and to exist in the space that is the Otherworld."

Nia asked the obvious before I could. "Is the power the Morrigan gave Claire enough? Or is that why—" They gestured at the gathering of midwitches and Crones around the worn harvest table that dominated the kitchen.

"That is why," Keven agreed.

"Wait." I frowned. "You told me before that Morok couldn't cross into the Otherworld as long as he was attached to Merlin's body. How will my body cross?"

"I should have been more specific. He could not be forced across, but if he had been willing, it might have been different."

Might have didn't carry quite the reassurance I would have liked, but before I could pursue the uncertainty, Natalie spoke up.

"And once she's there?" she asked. "How do we know the power will be enough for her to survive?"

There was a long, heavy pause before the gargoyle answered. "We don't."

"And without our help, she won't be able to open the door to get back."

Keven's stony gaze met mine and held it as she shook her head. "No."

Fuck, I thought, watching the possibility of my survival devolve further.

"Not even when she rescues Lucan?" Natalie pressed, a note of panic entering her voice.

Keven continued to look at me without answering, as if waiting for—what? My own panic? I considered the possibility, but when I searched inside myself, I found ... nothing. No surprise, no panic, no fear. Nothing. I didn't know if I was ready for whatever was coming, but I did know that there was no alternative. I would do this because it needed to be done, and because no one else could even come close. But first ...

"So," I said to Keven. "How do we find this door?"

"CONFLUENCE," MUTTERED MAUREEN INTO THE SILENCE. WE were sitting around the battered harvest table in the kitchen again—the only place that could accommodate all of us—and the spaces in the discussion of where to find the door to the Otherworld had been growing longer and longer with each failed suggestion.

Ten pairs of tired eyes turned to Maureen. Keven had done her best to make everyone comfortable the night before, but between a lack of beds, makeshift mattresses on hard floors, and the many, many things on all our minds, there had been little sleep. And Keven being Keven, we had only herbal tea instead of the coffee we all desperately needed.

"Come again?" said Nia.

"Confluence," Maureen repeated, a little louder this time.

"What about it?"

But even as Nia asked the question, a tiny glimmer of an idea flitted around the edges of my mind, like one of the Wards that guarded the house. Confluence, the idea agreed, but it didn't say why. Before I could chase after it, Anne slammed her hand on the tabletop with enough force to make her teacup bounce—along with everyone in their respective seats.

"Confluence!" She jumped to her feet and waved both hands in the air. "Of course!"

Confusion clouded the expressions around the table, and raised eyebrows became furrowed instead.

"Um …" One of the midwitches who had arrived with Natalie raised a tentative hand—Colleen, maybe? Or Shelley? Natalie had introduced them, but my brain seemed to have dismissed names as nonessential, and I could remember none of them. Small wonder, with everything else that occupied my attention at the moment.

"What about it?" maybe-Colleen-or-Shelley asked.

The idea teasing along the edges of my mind coalesced with a suddenness that made me jump to my feet, too. "A meeting place!" I exclaimed. "The three rivers!"

Confusion still clouded the faces of the midwitches and Natalie, but both Nia and Elysabeth's expressions cleared as if a magical cloth had wiped across them—which it figuratively had—and Nia's mouth formed a perfect "o."

"A place of power," they whispered, repeating the words I recalled Anne once saying. Once, when we'd thought that Kate was still Kate and Morok was still Morok and everything had been—well, if not simple, then at least simpler.

Ish.

"Connecting land, water, and sky," Anne agreed. "And maybe more."

More, such as the Otherworld. I looked over at Keven, who was parceling up herbs in string-tied paper packages and tucking them into Edie's old rucksack in preparation for my journey. The strong scent of heal-all permeated the kitchen. She was making an extra-large packet of that one, I noticed.

"Keven? Could that be it?" I asked. "Could that be the door?"

The gargoyle grunted. "You may be right. But where exactly?"

"The cave," Natalie and I spoke together.

"Behind the waterfall," Natalie added. "Two rivers meet above it and flow together into the third. There's a cave behind the waterfall. We were there with Braden the summer before last. Remember, Maman? It felt ..." She trailed off, and the light in her eyes dimmed a little.

"Magickal?" Maureen supplied, her entire expression glowing with excitement and anticipation as she leaned across the table, looking between me and Natalie.

My daughter-in-law shook her head, then shrugged. "Maybe?" she said. Then, "No, it was more ..." She looked at me for help and I shivered, remembering that day all too well. The warmth of the sun, the roar of water tumbling over the rocks, the cool spray on my face as we passed beneath the curtain into the cavern beyond, and the way the very air itself seemed to thicken as we ventured further in.

"Hostile," I said, lowering myself back down onto the bench. The wood dug into the back of my knees, and I tried and failed to focus on the discomfort of that rather than the discomfort of my thoughts. "It felt hostile. Like it didn't want us there."

I had been only too happy to leave that afternoon—and I didn't relish a return there now.

All around the table, Crones and midwitches alike let out long exhales. Anne was the first to speak. "So. That's it then," she said quietly. "That's the place we're looking for."

But she didn't sound happy about the idea, and when I lifted my eyes to meet hers, I found them filled with a compassion and knowledge that was reflected in every other face around the table, except for Natalie's, which simply looked stricken.

My nebulous death sentence had just moved up to imminent.

CHAPTER 5

WE MOVED INTO OUR PREPARATIONS WITH QUIET EFFICIENCY, wasting no time because—although no one spoke the thought aloud—there was no time *to* waste. We had no idea how long it would take us to get me into the Otherworld, or how long it would take me to traverse it and find Camlann—or to find Morgana's magick—or, or, or.

The uncertainties were endless. My courage in the face of them was not. Especially after the final bombshell Keven had dropped on me as the others filed from the kitchen.

"Milady, there is one more thing," she'd said, her voice pitched low as her clunky fingers tied string around another packet of herbs with surprising dexterity. "The Otherworld is not our world. Your magick ..."

"What about my magick?"

"You mustn't use it."

"I—what?" I'd gaped at her. "Why not?"

"The elements there might not be the same as they are here. There's no way of knowing how they will respond—or if they will at all. Or worse, what you might—" She'd looked over her shoulder at the doorway and pitched her voice low, so that no one still in the corridor would hear. Except Bedivere, of course, because I had no doubt he waited for me there, and he heard everything.

"What you might attract if you try," the gargoyle had finished heavily, and her words had rocked to the core what little foundation had remained beneath me.

I distracted myself from them—and from all the rest of the impossibilities facing me—as best I could. I couldn't help the Crones and midwitches with their ritual preparation, so I walked with Natalie through the woods to the road where she'd left her car and waved goodbye when she drove off. She'd insisted that Paul and Braden should see me before I left, and I hadn't had the strength to deny her.

"Closure is important, remember?" she whispered in my ear as she hugged me tight. "Paul would never forgive me—or you—if he ... if you ... you know what I mean."

I did. And I knew she was right—from Paul's perspective. From mine, however ...

My throat closed over just thinking about how strong I'd have to stay for my son when I said goodbye to him. And my heart shriveled at the thought of seeing Braden now and at the possibility of not seeing him again—at all of it.

But I smiled and nodded when Natalie rolled down her window to say yet again, "Three hours. At the waterfall parking lot. And I'll see if Jeanne will come, too."

"Three hours," I agreed, because it was what I had to do.

She drove away in a spurt of gravel, and I turned back toward the house. Bedivere had followed me as he always did, but he'd hung back at the gate while I'd walked Natalie to her car. He fell into step beside me as I passed between the stone pillars.

"You don't have to do this," he muttered gruffly. "There's a chance Morok might not even find Morgana's magick."

I shot him a sideways look, surprised at the apparent change of heart from the person whose idea it had been in the first place to go after Lucan. "And if he does? If he opens the portal and returns here, then what?"

"We face him together. All of us."

"Him with more than half his powers back in addition to Morgana's magick," I said. "We wouldn't stand a chance, Bedivere. You know that."

The shifter fell silent, and for a few minutes, there was only the sound of our footsteps on the path between us. I found myself searching the trees, but the crows that had plagued me were gone. I gave a soft snort. Damned if I didn't miss the feathered harbingers.

"He might not be alive," Bedivere said.

We weren't talking about Morok anymore. I nodded. "I know."

The burly shifter put his one hand on my arm, drawing me to a stop at the edge of the clearing where the house sat. "Milady, if you go to Camlann and he's not there, you face Morok alone. If you do not find the magick before he does, you die alone. Here, you do not."

"I know that, too," I said, then I tilted my head to the side and frowned at him. "Why the change of heart? Ever since I got back, you've been pushing me to go after Lucan, and now you think I should stay. What gives?"

Bedivere's hand fell away from my arm, and he stared into the trees. "I didn't know about Morgana's magick then. I thought ..."

He didn't finish. He didn't need to. A flush of heat washed over me. Cold followed in its wake, and the sick hollowness of doubt settled again in my belly. So much for distracting myself. I gritted my teeth and lifted my chin.

"You thought I had a chance," I finished, my voice harsh in my own ears. "And now you don't."

The shifter didn't disagree. Instead, he changed tactics. "Lucan would never forgive me if I allowed you to do this, milady."

Guilt threaded through his voice, and his words tried to share it with me. Once, not so long ago, I would have accepted it. Hesitated. Wavered. Now, however, I sidestepped it, because quite simply, it didn't belong to me. I couldn't— wouldn't—be responsible for his feelings—

"He has feelings?" my Edie-voice muttered in my head. A tiny smile quirked at the side of my mouth, but I smoothed it away and finished my thought. I couldn't be responsible for Bedivere's feelings any more than I could be for anyone else's.

Not right now. Not if I didn't want to fold under their weight. Not if I was going to do this.

I lifted my chin higher and squared my shoulders under my cloak. Then I cleared my throat and waited for the shifter's gaze to meet mine. I held it without wavering.

"It isn't Lucan's decision to make, Bedivere," I said. "And it's not yours, either."

BACK AT THE HOUSE, I DID WHAT I SHOULD HAVE DONE WEEKS before and focused my energies on the house itself—and its occupants—that I would be leaving behind.

The midwitches would return to their own lives, but I suspected that the Crones would remain, at least for a while. I wanted to be sure that they and Keven—and yes, Bedivere, too—were looked after. That the house would shelter them in my absence, even if that meant ... well.

And if the Crones and Bedivere eventually moved on, as they likely would, I wanted to know that Keven would always have the house—and that the house would have Keven. I couldn't bear the thought of either of them existing alone for eternity.

I wandered from room to room, upstairs and down, and had a long heart-to-heart with the last of the Crone houses—the only one to have survived Morok and his Mages.

"I'm sorry," I whispered to it in the sitting room. "I know you're tired. I am, too. But we're not done yet, you and I. I need you. *They* need you."

I continued into the front hall, trailing my hand along the walls, repeating my words, urging the structure to breathe, to come back to itself, to care again as it once had. I promised it that the battle this time would take place far away, and that the others would love and appreciate it as it deserved.

At last, with much coaxing, the house stirred. I felt it shift beneath my touch as my fingers traced the stones of the upstairs corridor wall, again as they followed the curving line of the banister on my way back down to the main floor. Walls creaked and groaned, ceilings lifted a little higher, and light filtered through windows that cleared of dust and grime. It wasn't much, but it was a start. The house alone could do more now, and I could only hope that it would.

I saved the cellar for last. Wall sconces sprang to life as I descended the stairs to where I had taken my magick lessons with Keven and we'd learned that I could connect with all four of the elements rather than the one expected.

I smiled at the memory of rooting myself to the floor—and the one where I'd nearly blown the gargoyle off her feet with the storm I'd conjured. I paused at the bottom of the stairs and let my gaze travel the room carved from stone. It rested on a crack in the floor. It had been there that my wand had taken root and grown into a linden tree—a tree that had protected me and died for me in my first battle with the Mages, and then had yielded the staff that Lucan had carved for me.

I crossed the cellar and knelt on the cool, smooth stone. I traced my fingers over the fissure. I would take the staff with me, of course. I had no idea what I would face in the Other-world, or if the staff would be helpful against any of it, but I would find comfort in having it with me. In the fact that Lucan's hands had once held it, too, and that Keven had given me the original wand from which it had come.

Comfort in knowing that I carried with me at least the memories of my friends.

"Milady?" Keven called down the stairs. "The others are ready."

I closed my eyes and breathed deeply of the cool air that smelled of earth and stone and ... home. I held the air in my lungs for a second, then released it in a slow exhale.

"Milady?"

"Coming," I said. I pushed to my feet and scanned the room one last time, memorizing it. Imprinting the memories on my every cell. Holding it in my center. Then I turned toward the stairs.

Keven was waiting for me in the corridor when I emerged from the cellar. She held the rucksack in her hands.

"I packed food," she said. "As much as I could fit in with the herbs."

"Thank you," I said. I reached for it, but she shook her head and held it out of reach.

"It's heavy. I'll help you."

I stood quietly as she slipped the strap over my head and settled it onto my right shoulder, then fussed with adjusting the bag at my back. Not until it rested as she thought it should did she step away.

"There," she said, her voice gruffer than normal. "You should be comfortable with that."

"It's fine," I said. "Thank you."

"The others are waiting in the front hall."

I looked down the corridor past her shoulder and nodded, but the gargoyle put out a hand to stop me from passing.

"Before you go," she said, "you must have wondered."+

Wondered—oh dear goddess, of course. "The magick!" I exclaimed. "When I get there—to Camlann—where will I find it? Where did the Morrigan put it?"

Keven seemed as surprised by the question as I'd been to realize I hadn't already asked. "I didn't tell you?"

I shook my head, and she shrugged her bunched-muscle shoulders.

"I do not know, milady, and the Morrigan—the Morrigan does not remember."

My mouth dropped open. "I'm sorry? How in hell did she forget something like that?"

"The memory stayed behind in the splinter." Keven sighed. "With me. With Morgana."

For a long moment, I stared at the gargoyle, trying to absorb this new revelation. She was kidding. She had to be kidding. But her expression said otherwise, and there was a certain logic behind her words. When Morok's powers had been split by the splinter magick, he himself had still come through to this world in the body of Merlin. But the Morrigan had left Morgana's form there, in the Camlann splinter, and—

"But that was not what I meant," Keven said.

"What?" I looked up at her uncomprehendingly, my brain still occupied with the Morrigan-forgetting puzzle.

"When I said you must have wondered, I meant about why I didn't tell you about Morok and my magick sooner."

I had wondered, I remembered. But the question had paled in the face of the information itself. "I'm sure you had your reasons," I said. "And really, it doesn't mat—"

"It does matter," the gargoyle growled, so fiercely that I took a surprised step back. "It matters because you once claimed me as friend, milady, and I denied you. I shouldn't have done that."

"I—" I broke off, not knowing how to respond to that.

"I didn't tell you because I have had few friends in my life," Keven continued, "even before ... this." A massive hand moved up and down along her torso in an encompassing gesture. "You and the mutt have reminded me not just of what it means to have a friend, but of what it means to lose one, too. I didn't tell you, milady, because I didn't want to lose you, too."

I looked up at the granite figure looming over me. At the heavy brow, the mastiff-like muzzle, the four prominent, curved teeth protruding from her jaw, the stocky body set on heavily muscled legs. She seemed incomplete without the ever-present orange cat draped across her shoulders, but Gus had been nowhere to be found when we were leaving the house. I'd looked for him, wanting to give him one last scratch behind the ears and see him stretch his forelegs out luxuriously in response. Even if he had abandoned me long ago in favor of Keven, I still thought of him as my cat, and I would miss him, too. Him, and Keven, and the Crones, and—

And of all the things I might have expected the gargoyle to say, this would have been furthest from my mind. It wouldn't have so much as entered it. Nor would I have expected to find moisture welling at the corner of granite eyes when I moved to stand in front of her so that she had no choice but to look at me.

"I don't—I—" I stopped, unable to find the words I wanted. The words she needed.

I wanted to tell her that I would be back and that she wouldn't lose me, but those were lies, and she deserved more from me. Better. I wanted to tell her that she would be okay without me, but with no more Crones in her future, she wouldn't lose just a friend, she would lose her purpose.

And without purpose, no one was okay.

I wanted to tell her all that and more, but if the words existed, I couldn't find them and so I wrapped my arms around the stone torso and laid my head on the unyielding shoulder and simply held her. After long seconds, granite arms lifted and went around me, gentle and careful in their return hug.

"Forgive me?" she rumbled beneath my ear.

"There is nothing to forgive," I said—and those words, I knew to be true. Because while the secrets she had kept from me may have given Morok more time, blame had no place here. What was done was done, and now there was only forward. I would undo what I could, save what I could, and love with all my heart in what time I had left.

Starting with my irascible, cranky gargoyle.

A long, shuddering sigh went through the stone against

me, and then her chest rumbled beneath my ear again. "You should go, milady. You have only a few hours before dark."

"Claire," I corrected. I made my voice fierce, because if I didn't, it would break, and then so would I. "My name is Claire, and yours is—"

"Keven," she said. She set me away from her and picked up my staff from where it was propped against the wall. She pushed it into my hands. The moisture I'd seen at the corners of her eyes was gone. "I am Keven. And I am honored to have been your friend, Claire Emerson."

CHAPTER 6

WE TRAVELED A LEY LINE TO THE FALLS WHERE THE THREE rivers of Confluence met. Bedivere scouted ahead to identify the one that would take us there, and the Crones and midwitches had gathered beside it in a tight circle with their arms intertwined. Then, with the shifter standing outside their perimeter, his own arms outstretched as if to encompass them all and my left hand grasping his only one, I had reached into the Earth and gathered the elemental power there, using it to extend his protective energy around them. I had nodded to Bedivere, he had taken a single step backwards into the ley line, and we had all followed.

It had been almost effortless, and for a single, brief instant when we arrived beside the waterfall, I wondered if I might perhaps have enough power to defeat Morok after all. If I might *be* enough.

But as I watched the others silently pick their way along the shore and disappear behind the curtain of water, my brief satisfaction gave way to the cold, hard reality of not knowing if we could even find the door to the Otherworld, let alone open it. Or if I would survive the trek through that world or find Camlann. Or—

"One step at a time," my Edie-voice said. *"You'll drive yourself crazy if you think too far ahead."*

"Too late," I muttered. "I think I'm already there."

"Milady?" asked Bedivere.

"Sorry, just talking to myself again."

"I'm used to that. I was referring to this." He held up his hand with mine still attached to it.

Oh, yeah. If I hadn't noticed I still held the shifter's hand,

35

I was definitely already there, all right. I sighed as I freed his fingers from my grasp. "Sorry about that."

He ignored the apology and nodded toward the parking lot on the other side of the leafless bushes. "I hear vehicles coming. You must say your farewells."

I nodded. "You should go with the others. Tell them Natalie and I will be there in a few minutes."

Bedivere frowned suspiciously at our surroundings. "I don't care to leave you here on your own."

"I can look after myself," I promised. "I'll have to where I'm going, remember?"

The shifter's frown became a scowl and words devolved into a grunt, but he didn't follow me when I started toward the parking area, and when I glanced back, he was gone. For a moment, the solitude closed in on me, but then I, too, heard the crunch of tires on gravel. I braced myself for what was to come.

Farewells, Bedivere had said. I mulled over the word as I picked my way between shrubby willows and a patch of wild raspberry canes with a handful of brittle leaves clinging to them. It didn't feel weighty enough for this situation. Farewell sounded light and bright: fare well, stay safe, have fun …

But what about when you were saying goodbye forever? When you knew, in your heart of hearts, that you were never going to hug your son again, never going to breathe in the scent of your grandson as you held him close, never going to watch them grow or change or live, never feel their joy … and not even witness their sorrow when they realized you wouldn't be returning.

I stepped clear of the tangle of dormant vegetation and onto the rough gravel parking area as Natalie's little red car and Paul's black SUV both pulled up in front of me. Natalie emerged from the car and opened the back door to free Braden from his booster seat. Paul remained in the SUV, hands gripping the steering wheel as he stared through the windshield at me, shock, disbelief, and denial all playing across his features.

There was, as I had expected, no Jeanne. True to her declaration after she'd handed over the Book of the Fifth Crone to me, she'd wanted nothing to do with my magick. Or her own.

I held Paul's gaze through the windshield until Braden's arms wrapped around my legs and demanded my attention.

I had expected every second of every moment to burn itself into my memory. I thought I would be hyperaware of smells and touches and words and voices. I wanted the memories of these last moments—indelible, precious memories—to be written into my heart and soul. I got none of that.

Instead, I saw and felt and heard everything as if from a distance. As if an uncrossable chasm existed between me and my family. As if *I* were an uncrossable chasm.

When Paul got out of the vehicle and joined us, he held me tightly, the way he'd done when he was a boy. "Freaking hell, Mom," he whispered into my hair, his chin resting on the top of my head. "Why you? How did this even happen?"

But I had no words, no explanation that would be more than what Natalie had already given him, and no way to communicate the lifetime of love I had for him but couldn't seem to feel anymore. All I could do was return his embrace with wooden arms and hope that it would be enough. That he would remember our farewell—there was that word again—with something more than the grief in his eyes now.

From a long way away, I felt a tug on my pant leg and looked down at Braden again.

"Here, Grandma." He pressed something into my hand. "It's Thor. He'll pertect you against the dragons and things. Can I skip rocks now, Daddy? Can you come teach me again?"

"In a minute, buddy." Paul ruffled his son's hair. "Just give me a—"

"Go," I heard myself say. Fingers that were mine but not mine patted my son's arm as the me that wasn't me stepped away from his touch. "There's no point in drawing this out. Go. Look after your son. Teach him to skip stones."

For a second, I thought Paul would refuse, but then his shoulders hunched, and he nodded.

"Be careful, okay?" he said. "And come back? We love you."

"I love you, too," distant-me said. She even managed a smile, and then Paul was hugging his wife and making her promise to be careful, too, and saying that he would see her soon, and then he and Braden were taking an easier path through the bush to the shoreline and searching for the perfect skipping stones as they walked further downriver, and—

I took a step to follow them, suddenly, desperately needing to fold my grandson into my arms. Natalie touched my wrist. "Are you okay, Maman?"

I stumbled, and for a second, distant-me threatened to shatter into a million tiny pieces and take my scant protection with it. I couldn't let it. I didn't dare. I shored up the facade and wrapped it around me again. None of us could afford having me come apart at the seams right now, least of all me. Not with what lay ahead.

"I'm fine," I lied to my daughter-in-law, tucking the Thor figurine into the bottom of my rucksack. "Let's go."

CHAPTER 7

I PICKED MY WAY CAREFULLY BEHIND NATALIE, STAFF CLUTCHED in one hand and the other hand feeling its way along the stone wall of the cavern, cold and wet with mist from the waterfall. I'd looked back at Braden and Paul a few times, but now that we had passed under the curtain of water, I could no longer see them, and I needed all my focus to navigate the spray-slicked rocks.

It would be a hell of a thing to have come this far, only to find myself needing to be rescued by the local emergency services because I'd slipped and fallen into the river.

Ahead of me, Natalie kept glancing back over her shoulder, not at me but as if looking for something. Twice, uneasily, I followed her gaze. But there was nothing in the shadows behind us, and I decided that it was just her nerves. And no wonder, with everything she'd already been through. Everything we'd *all* been through.

It wasn't supposed to be like this, I thought numbly as I felt my way along, moving deeper into the cavern carved out over the centuries. Women my age weren't supposed to randomly go off to other worlds to fight gods with magick they'd never wanted in the first place, knowing they might never—*would* never—return. Women my age were supposed to meet friends for coffee and laughs; to have their families over for Sunday dinners; to read stories to their grandchildren and show them how to look for pictures in the clouds and watch them grow up, and—

A sudden force slammed into my chest, driving the air from me in a whoosh. My fingers skated over the slippery wall as I staggered backwards, scrambling for balance. The force shoved again, and then again, stronger each time. I grabbed for a small outcrop and clung to it with all my strength, staff raised to strike whatever was there, but I could see nothing. Ahead of me, Natalie continued forward, unaware of my invisible foe. It clearly didn't care about her presence in the—

Whatever it was shoved me again, and this time, a moist warmth brushed against my cheek like a breath, scented with earth and damp and decay. My heart rate kicked up several notches and I pressed back against the wall.

It just as clearly cared a great deal about *my* presence.

A half-dozen yards ahead, Natalie again turned to look for me.

"Maman?"

The waterfall was quieter here, and her voice carried easily to me. I opened my mouth to answer her, but the force pushed once more, hard enough to make me grunt, and this time, it didn't ease. It pressed against the length of my body— shoulders, chest, thighs—and the fetid warmth against my face was unmistakably breath. I gagged and recoiled, but with my back already to the wall, I had nowhere to go. The pressure against me increased, crushing me against the rock, and I gave silent thanks for the rucksack I wore. The food Keven had packed into it for me might not survive, but with its cushioning, my ribs might.

"Maman!" Alarm tinged Natalie's voice.

A hiss of anger accompanied another gust of air against my cheek, and the stench almost felled me. Through sheer determination, I made myself inhale and then yelled, "Go, Natalie! Now! Send Bedivere!"

Through a wavering distortion in the air between us, I saw her step toward me, hesitate, and curl her hands into fists in front of her as though she considered attack. Then, to my immense relief, because I'd stopped breathing and didn't think I could find enough air in my lungs to call out to her again, she turned and scurried into the dark.

I turned my full attention to my attacker. My staff was

wedged between me and it, so I wriggled until I could grip it with both hands, then I shoved against my foe as hard as I could. The force holding me against the wall eased for a millisecond, then returned—and then it took shape. My stunned brain cataloged it as rapidly as possible while also searching for escape.

The face that thrust itself into mine held black eyes with neither irises nor whites. Instead, they were only pupils—bottomless pupils that lacked expression, warmth, or even cold of any kind. Heavily lined features were so filthy they might have been made from dirt itself, and antlers, like those of a deer but thicker and shorter, sprouted from the temples. A symbol I didn't recognize had either been carved into or grew in the center of a forehead that was punctuated by a long, prominent nose beneath it. And around the face hung feculent hair, so entwined with grass and twigs that I thought for a moment it was entirely made of those.

All in all, it was a distinctly masculine face, but it wasn't human, especially not with clumps of sod and muck dropping with every movement. Not human and—judging by the bared, rotting teeth—not happy to have me here.

As for escape, I saw none.

"*Brddgh gfsff ddsfgh!*" the creature growled at me, one hand pinning mine to the wall, and the other arm pressed across my throat.

I recoiled from the spittle that sprayed my face and tried not to gag. Or to ask when it—he—had last brushed his teeth.

"Please. I'm not looking for trouble," I said. "I just want to get past and join my fr—"

"*Gztt!*" he spat. A clump of soil fell from his cheek, briefly exposing pale bone beneath before more soil filled the hole and revulsion filled me.

A zombie. He's a freaking horned zombie, freshly risen from his grave.

I closed my eyes and tried to rein in the encroaching hysteria bubbling up in my throat in the form of a cackle. The arm across my throat compressed harder, cutting off both cackle and air, and my eyes flew open again. I struggled against the creature's hold, grabbing at the arm that threatened to squeeze the life from me. It gave not an inch. Rising panic tangled with my hysteria—and then Lucan's cool voice in my memory replaced both.

"If you panic, you're dead," he said, and with a shock of clarity, I remembered. I remembered the training he'd insisted I do in case I wasn't able to access my magick. Remembered the times he'd held me in a lock of some kind and how he'd demanded I free myself. Remembered that I *had* freed myself. Remembered how.

I also remembered my damned magick.

Without warning, I let my knees sag, becoming a dead (and not inconsiderable) weight that slid down the wall and out of the creature's grasp. In the same instant, I swung my staff in a wide arc that connected with what I assumed were legs beneath a garment of moss and sticks. The creature grunted in surprise and went down like a sack of unwashed potatoes. Before he could recover or regain his feet, I scrambled to mine, slammed the end of my staff against the stone beneath us, and connected to Earth. Then I stretched out my hand and—

And nothing.

I stared at my feet in shock. I could feel their connection to Earth, but it was so faint that I could draw no magick from it. And it was … moving. Away from me and into—

My attention shot back to the creature. No. Not a creature. Not a zombie, either. He was nothing less than a goddamned—pardon the choice of words—*god*. I forced my thoughts to slow down and take in his details again. Properly this time. The moss robes, the skin made of Earth itself, the symbol—no, that was a rune—carved on his forehead ...

The antlers.

The antlers sealed it, and full understanding dawned alongside growing dread.

Cernunnos. He was fucking Cernunnos, the horned god, sometimes depicted as the Green Man—and he was tied to Earth itself.

The element flowed into and out of him as he laughed an ugly laugh and climbed back to his feet. He reached with one hand for the arm I still held outstretched, curling his other hand into a fist at his side. The Earth element's rush away from me intensified, and I felt its power swelling behind his touch. He raised his fist and drew it back, and I closed my eyes, bracing for an impact I couldn't survive. An impact that would end my quest before it had even be—

A snarling ball of furred fury slammed into the god and knocked him sideways. Cernunnos's grip on my arm relaxed, but it didn't release. He pulled me, staggering, in his wake, and I fought to stay on my feet as he fell to one knee. The ball of fury landed a dozen feet away and whirled, crouched for another attack. My heart leapt in my chest.

Bedivere.

But against a god with his full powers? My spark of hope guttered like a drowning candle. The shifter didn't have a chance, and I was still going to—

Wait.

Hope flared again. Heat flared beside it. Because Cernunnos might be tied to Earth, but I ... I was not.

I reacted before the thought had taken full form. Instinctively, I released the last of my connection to the Earth element, seized the Fire in my center, and fanned it into the mother of all hot flashes. With his attention divided between me and the threatening wolf-shifter, the god didn't notice. The heat spread through my entire body until it threatened to consume me, and then I drew it inward again, funneled it down the arm Cernunnos still grasped, and let it roll over him in a ball of fire so intense that the stone beneath his feet cracked.

It might have been overkill, but he *was* a god and I only had half of the Morrigan's powers, and—

The horned god, his robes and hair ablaze with blue flames, struggled to his feet and I quailed beneath his roar of pure, unadulterated rage. Well, shit, I thought. So much for overkill. Another hand seized my shoulder and spun me around.

"*Run!*" Bedivere growled.

He shoved me in the direction Natalie had taken, and I didn't argue. Hiking my cloak clear of my ankles, I sidestepped the flaming god and belted after Natalie with all the speed my adrenaline-fueled, sixty-year-old legs could summon.

CHAPTER 8

BETWEEN GASPS FOR AIR—I WAS *SO* NOT A RUNNER—I COULD
hear women's voices raised in chant up ahead. There was
nothing graceful about my flight toward them. With no light
and no time to call one, I stumbled and slid along the path,
slipping on the rocks and falling twice. My rucksack, its strap
loosened in the struggle, flapped and banged against my backside, spurring me on. Cernunnos's bellows of rage and Bedivere's answering wolf-snarls behind me did the same.

By the time I reached the back of the cavern, my lungs
were heaving like bellows, I'd put my foot through the fabric
of my cloak twice, and my hands and knees were all scraped
raw.

But I'd made it. I'd found the others, and ... and momen-
tary awe slowed my steps as I took in the Crones and
midwitches who stood in a semi-circle before the cavern's back
wall. Daylight had no chance of making it this far back, and
there were no cracks or crevices where it could creep through,
but the natural, low-ceilinged room glowed with a pale green
light for which no source existed. It was unearthly, I thought,
and then I shivered at my choice of words, all too fitting given
what we'd come in search of.

The women's arms stretched high above their heads as
they chanted, and their voices rose and fell in a cadence unfa-
miliar to me, as so much of their magick was because I still
knew so little—and now likely always would. But whatever I
did or didn't know of the witchcraft they (with the exception
of Natalie) had studied for years didn't matter. It mattered
only that it was working, that they worked to raise their
magick together—for me, for Lucan if he still lived, for the

world. I could feel their power pulsating through air and stone alike, and I felt an answering stir within me.

Beyond the semi-circle, a faint outline shimmered in the cavern wall, and my heart skipped a beat. That was it. We'd been right. We'd found the door to the Otherworld.

It was time. Urgency tugged at me, but I hesitated. The distant-me who had said goodbye to Paul and Braden had long since disappeared—probably choked out of existence by Cernunnos—and all the feelings and fears that I'd held at bay flooded back. In spades.

My breathing turned ragged for reasons other than sprinting through the cavern, because this was it. This was my last chance to change my mind. Once I joined the others, once I stepped into their magick and joined with it and the door opened, there would be no turning back. There would be no more Crones or midwitches, no more Keven or Gus, no more surly Bedivere, no more Paul or Braden or Natalie. I would be on my own, well and truly on my own as I never had been, and I would have to—

A roar sounded behind me, and an animal screamed in pain. My heart twisted, and the breath hissed from my lungs. *Bedivere*. The cavern trembled with the thunder of approaching footsteps. *Cernunnos*.

The women in the circle faltered in their chant.

Fuck.

I caught Anne's eye as the green glow flickered and began to wane. "Keep going," I shouted. She glanced toward the approaching commotion, then nodded and raised her voice over it. Rallying, the others joined in.

I shifted the rucksack's strap on my shoulder so that its weight sat more firmly behind me, gripped my staff, and willed myself to turn and face the god storming into the cavern. I could hold him at bay for a few minutes, while the Crones and midwitches finished raising their magick, but then what? How could I keep him back at the same time as I joined the circle and opened the door?

And how, in the name of the goddess, could I keep the others safe from him once I'd stepped through that door?

Cernunnos thudded to a stop before me and pointed a begrimed finger at me. *"Gzbdrrgh!"* he spat, his black eyes glowing red.

Jesus fuck, I thought in reply as bits of I-didn't-want-to-know-what flew from his mouth and landed on my cheek. But I swallowed my gag and held my stance, feet wide and shoulders back, staff planted against the floor. I even lifted my chin for good measure. "I have no choice," I told him. "I have to go through. The Morrigan—"

"Zbfg rfdrgh!" the horned god screeched.

Okay, so he wasn't a fan of the goddess.

I tried again. "Morok—"

The screech this time was unintelligible as even an attempt at speech, and half of Cernunnos's bottom jaw splattered against the front of my cloak. I wasn't going to be able to reason my way out of this.

Cernunnos spread his arms wide and held them up in a *v*, palms cupped toward the ceiling. He lifted a bare, dirt-encrusted foot and slammed it down against the stone floor. A tremor ran through the cavern. He did the same with his other foot. The tremor became a rumble, and pebbles fell from the ceiling. A third slam. Pebbles became fist-sized rocks, and dawning terror filled me.

He intended to bury us. Even if I still had a chance to get through the door to the Otherworld—and that possibility became fainter by the second—he would still bury the others, and I wouldn't be able to stop him, and—

The horned god staggered forward a step as something hit him from behind. I glimpsed fur and caught my breath on a surge of hope. Bedivere. Bedivere had survi—

My recognition dropped off the edge of a cliff into pity. Horror. Disbelief. Oh dear goddess. *Bedivere.*

The burly shifter was in man form ... but not. His face was elongated but not all the way into a muzzle, and canine teeth protruded from what was still a human mouth. He had the gray eyes of his wolf, and a wolf's ears clung to the sides of his head, and fur-covered patches on his bare torso, and legs that were undeniably those of an animal, but his hands ... his remaining hand ... the only one he'd had left ...

I knew what he'd done, then. Knew what he'd lost and what it cost him.

The scream of pain we'd heard—that had been Cernunnos taking his one remaining hand. The shifter could run on three legs, but not on two. Not in his full wolf-form. Somehow he'd transitioned halfway, caught himself between man and wolf the way the goliath had been caught between wolf and gargoyle, and had returned to fight the horned god. And it would a fight to the death, because blood streamed from the shifter's arm, and he swayed and staggered as if determination alone could hold him up. It couldn't.

Cernunnos swung his own arm, and the back of his hand caught Bedivere full in the chest with a thud that reverberated hollowly through the chamber. The shifter grunted, flew through the air, slammed into the cavern wall, and collapsed in a silent, unmoving heap. I took an instinctive step toward him, wanting—needing—to help. But something wiser than me held me back. Held me still. Made me look back to the semi-circle of Crones and midwitches. Made me inhale in hope, exhale in despair.

Because in the few seconds Bedivere had bought for them, the witches had completed their spell. Their magick veritably hummed through the stone room, and the outline in the back wall glowed fiercely. Undeniably. Ominously.

They'd done it. The witches had found the door, and now they—and it—called for me.

"Claire!" Nia called. "Now!"

The horned god swung away from the crumpled Bedivere, his gaze skipping over me in search of the voice. It settled on the witches, and what little air remained in my lungs turned to shards of ice. In an instant, I saw what would happen if I opened the door and went through to the Otherworld. I knew, absolutely and without doubt, that I would sentence all of the women here to inescapable death. And I saw in their grim, determined faces that they knew, too.

The indecision of grief cemented my feet to the stone floor. Natalie—Braden—

Once again, a child's voice wailed in my memory, *"Mama-mamamama!"* My heart shattered anew, and its agony spread through my chest, my veins, my belly and—

A flash of light arced through the cavern, the air sizzling in its wake. Cernunnos roared and stumbled backward, his skin also sizzling. He recovered quickly and once more spread his hands wide over his head, but before he could strike foot against rock, another arc of light landed on him, and then another and another and another, each driving him a step back and wringing a bellow from him.

Shock elbowed my grief aside. I knew those arcs of light. I'd seen them before, when—I blinked. Wait, those were *hexes*, and the only person I'd seen throw them was—

"Go!" a familiar voice called. "I'll hold him back for you!"

I gaped at the figure emerging from the shadows into the cavern, long fingers dancing in the air, tracing sigils, launching another blast at the horned god.

"Jeanne?"

Jeanne, my former neighbor and friend, neatly dressed as always in slacks and one of the crisp plaid shirts she favored, blasted another hex across the cavern. The burst of light smacked into the horned god, who had given up doing anything except try to defend himself from the barrage. But it wouldn't last. At some point, he was bound to regain his equilibrium, and when he did, I didn't think the last Daughter of Hestia would be able to stand up to the power of a god, and then Jeanne, too, would—

"Go," my old friend said again, glaring at me fiercely even as her fingers sketched another sigil. "You'll never have another chance, Claire. Open the door, damn it!"

She'd come through for me. I couldn't believe she'd come through for me.

I hitched up my soggy cloak and hefted my staff.

"What about them?" I asked, jutting my chin toward the others, the ones holding onto the magick they'd raised to make the door visible. The ones who would never get past Cernunnos on their own. The ones who included my daughter-in-law.

Calm brown eyes met mine from behind red plastic frames. "I'll get them out," Jeanne promised. "You have my word. Now, for the love of all that is holy, *go*."

I went.

CHAPTER 9

I HAD NO TIME TO THANK THE MIDWITCHES WHO HAD followed Natalie to the Earth house. No time to thank the women who had given up everything to battle Morok beside me as Crones and then again to stand against the guardian of the door to the Otherworld as midwitches, with only the power of their own magick at their disposal. No time to hug my daughter-in-law one last time or to whisper to her how much I loved her. Respected her. Believed in her.

Or to tell her how very sorry I was to have brought her into this.

I had no time for any of that as the circle parted to allow me to enter it, then closed around me with a warm familiarity. I hadn't raised the magick, but it recognized me nonetheless, and without hesitation, it gave me the catalyst I needed to open the door waiting for me. The focus.

I moved with intention, determination, purpose. First, I rooted my feet to the stone of the cavern floor and called on Earth. Then I found Fire in my core and fanned it high. I spread my arms wide and reached out with every atom of focus I possessed to connect to Air and Water. A gust of wind blew in from the waterfall we'd come through, carrying leaves and debris and a mist of water. It swirled into a whirlwind, gaining force with every rotation, until Crones and midwitches alike spread themselves flat on the cavern floor that was now bucking beneath them. It bucked beneath me, too, but I was part of it—part of it all—and I felt it only at the edges of my awareness as the elements came together in a maelstrom of power.

Somewhere behind me, Cernunnos roared in pain. Rage. Frustration.

I set the end of the staff against the stone floor and held it firmly. The power thrumming through the cavern floor crept up my legs, through my body, along my arm, and into the wood. Fire coursed through my veins, and its flames licked along the staff's length but did not char it. The water-bearing vortex that spun through the chamber grew smaller, until it encircled only me and the staff, then only the staff. The elements were united. They were ready.

Regret writhed in my chest like a trapped, wild animal, tearing a ragged breath that was half sob from me. With every atom of my being, I wanted to cast my gaze around the women—friends, family, and strangers alike—that I would be leaving behind. But I didn't dare, because if I did, I wasn't sure I could go through with this. So instead, with one hand, I gripped the strap of the rucksack Keven had given me that contained all that I would take with me from this world. With the other, I leveled the staff at the glowing wall and sent the power I'd gathered through it.

Bits of rock rained down as a thunderous rumble shook the cavern. The outline of the door in the wall glowed brighter but remained otherwise unchanged. Uncertainty gripped me. Had I misjudged? Done too much? Too little? Gotten it wrong altogether? Any of those were possible, but it wasn't like this task had come with any kind of instructions, and ...

Cernunnos bellowed behind me, and I gritted my teeth.

And sometimes, the only available form of transportation —especially if you are hoping to cross from one world into another—is a literal leap of faith. Or in this case, a headlong run at a wall that still looked to be awfully solid.

Before I could change my mind or let sanity prevail, I braced for impact and threw myself at said wall.

I DIDN'T HIT ROCK, EXACTLY, BUT NEITHER DID I PASS through to something else. Anything else. Instead, it felt like I'd run straight into the middle of a bowl of half-set, pitch black gelatin. It clung to my arms, my legs, my torso. It pressed in around my face, filling my ears and eyes and nostrils, and then my mouth when I instinctively gasped for air. I could see nothing, hear nothing ...

And when it slowly began to harden around me, I couldn't move, either.

Panic clawed at my chest and terror at the edges of my mind, and my brain stalled. Was this it? Was this the Otherworld, so inhospitable to humans that we died the moment we set foot in it? I would have sobbed from sheer despair, but I had no air for sobbing. No air for anything.

There were sparks of red light going off behind my eyeballs from lack of oxygen, and Jesus Christ on a cracker, after all of the effort I'd put into getting past Cernunnos and raising the magick to open the door, all of the sacrifices that had been made for me and that I had made, this was how I was going to go? In a cosmic bowl of gelatin? I tightened my grip on the staff I'd managed to hold onto.

Over my fucking dead body.

"No irony intended?" asked my Edie-voice.

Ignoring it, I dragged my free hand up along my body to my face and cleared a small space in front of it. I spat out the gelatin already in my mouth and carefully inhaled. Air— blessed, blessed air—crept down my throat and into my lungs. Battling the urge to suck for more, I leaned all my weight as far forward as I could and turned my attention to my feet. I dragged one of them an inch forward ... then two inches. Then I did the same with the other. Then I made my body lean forward again.

My rucksack tugged at my shoulder, trying to drag me back, and I considered abandoning it. But even if I could have managed to get it over my head, leaving it behind would have meant I had nothing. Nothing in the god world, nothing when —if—I got to Camlann.

And so, ignoring the cut of the bag's strap across my collarbone, I continued. Step. Step. Clear a space. Breathe. Step. Step. Clear.

Gradually, I found a rhythm. The leaning forward was the hardest part, but I discovered that if I moved steadily, without breaking pace, the gelatin—or whatever it was—gave way a little more easily, becoming less solid and more glutinous. Any satisfaction I felt at the discovery was short lived, however, because the resistance went on and on and on.

My tiny breaths became insufficient, and panic returned as my lungs demanded more air in return for fueling my efforts. Panic, agitation, the return of regret and despair ...

I shored up my dwindling reserves as best I could, but I was becoming increasingly sure that I wasn't going to make it out of here. I was going to die in the middle of a swamp of black gelatin, and no one would ever know that I hadn't made it to the Otherworld or found Camlann or Lucan or Morok or—

A sob tore at my throat and I hiccupped, drawing in a mouthful of goo. In a flash, terror won. I gasped for air and flailed at the morass trying to swallow me alive. Fuck, I thought as the gelatin closed around my legs, my staff, my arms, and began to harden again. Fuckity, fuck fuck *fuck*.

In a hopeless, last-ditch effort, I threw myself forward with all the strength I possessed. All the determination. All the rage at all the losses and sacrifices and—

And without warning, I pitched forward into clear, cold air. My eyes popped open onto darkness, my arms pinwheeled madly, and I fought for my balance. Fought for it, failed to find it, and promptly fell down what felt like the side of a tall, very rocky mountain.

CHAPTER 10

A GENTLE RUMBLE VIBRATED AGAINST MY CHEST, TUGGING ME from sleep. I smiled at the familiar weight of a cat and lifted a hand to stroke his—

Agony lanced through my wrist, then through my shoulder, then through the rest of me.

I opened my eyes and stared up at the branches of a winter-bare tree against a slate-gray sky—and then at Gus, narrow-eyed and loafing on my chest, which was about the only thing that didn't scream at me in pain. What in the name of the goddess had—

Memories of gelatin slammed into me, and then of my long, long, *long* fall down a ... mountain? Cautiously, I turned my head to the left, hissing at the objection from my neck. I blinked at the tree trunk beside me, and then shifted my gaze past it, to where the land continued to drop sharply away. I stared at the desolate landscape, empty of anything but a scattering of stones, an outcropping of rock here and there and, way down at the bottom—a very long way down—a thin, black ribbon running in a straight line across the base.

Well, hell. This was the Otherworld? *This?* Or had we landed in some *other* Other? Somewhere ...

My gaze went back to the ribbon, and my fogged brain trailed after it. A river, perhaps, it mused. Far enough away that it could take me days to make my way down to it. Unless, of course, I just threw myself down the remainder of the incline.

The very idea hurt, and I massaged the pain stabbing through my temple, then hissed out a breath at the accompanying stab in the wrist, then wondered at the weight on my chest and remembered seeing Gus when I opened my eyes and—

Gus?

This time I remembered the pain *before* I moved. I turned my head slowly, carefully, deliberately—until I was staring at the weight on my chest. It blinked orange eyes at me. I gaped back.

"It *is* you," I said. "But ... but *how?*"

Gus yawned and went back to his quiet rumbling. Still staring at him, half afraid he would disappear if I looked away, I began to piece things together.

I'd survived the gelatin. I'd fallen. I was in—I had no idea where I was. And Gus—*my* Gus—had somehow followed me. I sat with the summary—or lay with it, as the case was—and let it sink in for a moment. Two things rose to the surface, the most important ones: I was alive, and I had Gus. I could work with those, I decided.

I took a long, cautious breath. It wasn't what I'd call comfortable, but no serious stabs responded, and relief washed over me. My ribs were okay, then, which meant, I hoped, that there were no internal injuries, either. That was good, right? As for the rest of my limbs ...

I systematically flexed toes, ankles, knees, and hips, followed by fingers, my other wrist, and elbows and shoulders. There were various pinches and twinges and an overall feeling that the mountain had fallen on me rather than me down it, but all in all, the results of my assessment were promising. As in, I might eventually get myself upright again. Eventually. Right now, however, the mere act of taking stock of my body had exhausted me, and I wanted nothing more than to close my eyes and—

A fuzzy head butted the underside of my chin, and then a small, cold, wet nose touched mine. I groaned. I cracked an eye open and sighed at the cat sitting on me.

"You're right," I said. "At the very least, we should find somewhere more comfortable for a nap."

Gus slid off my chest and—when I didn't move fast enough to suit him—head-butted my ribs. My skin prickled. I focused my attention outward. Did he know something I didn't? Sense something I couldn't? I could hear nothing, but his ears were many times more acute than mine, and ...

I could hear nothing.

The realization gelled and the breath in my throat turned sour. I strained to listen harder, but ... nope. Nothing. Not so much as a whisper of sound. No wind, no birds, no anything. A frisson of unease slithered down my spine, and getting upright became imperative. I twisted my protesting body around, trying to roll it uphill to get from my back to my front. It would have been a great deal easier to roll the other way and let gravity help, but first, tree, and second, given the pitch of the slope, I wasn't at all sure I could stop my momentum.

It took everything I had in me, but at last I wriggled onto my front, then onto my knees and finally, with the aid of the tree beside me, onto two unsteady feet. Shaking with effort and dizzy with the pain from my right wrist and shoulder—because of course it had been my dominant arm that I'd injured—I rested my backside against the gnarled tree trunk and bent double at the waist. Sparks and stars glittered behind the eyelids I'd squeezed shut, and Gus's soft body wove in and out around my ankles.

A wave of nausea carried my belly contents into my chest. I gritted my teeth until it subsided, then I blew out a slow breath and pushed myself erect, my one good hand braced against a bruised thigh. With my eyes open again, I leaned tender shoulder blades and equally tender hips against the tree trunk and surveyed my situation. It did not look good.

My staff lay within reach, but the rucksack Keven had given me sat, empty and deflated, about thirty feet above from us on the hard ground. It might as well have been thirty miles, because crawling up there on my knees and one hand would be all but impossible. And that didn't include going after the packages that had spilled from it and were scattered across the slope. Packages I needed, especially the ones that contained the herbs Keven had packed for healing.

Because dear goddess, this arm of mine was going to need some healing.

I puffed out my cheeks in another breath, then winced at the burn along my jawline. I put my hand up to it, and my fingertips came away smeared with blood. Awesome. I wiped them on my torn, dirty cloak and surveyed the slope again, cringing at the thought of trekking back up it.

Fucking hell, but this hadn't gone as I'd expected.

Not that I'd had any idea what to expect in the first place, but if I'd had expectations, they wouldn't have been this.

Then my gaze dropped to Gus, now sitting and washing a paw at my feet.

"Gus, I don't suppose—"

The cat trotted up the mountain before I even finished and, while I was still blinking in surprise, seized the nearest string-wrapped package. With great delicacy—and far more grace than I could have mustered—he minced his way back down the slope, package bobbing against his chest. He laid it in the spot he'd vacated and left again, this time grabbing the strap of the rucksack itself. The empty bag didn't behave as well as the package had. It bounced against his back legs and overtook him twice, causing him to face-plant in the dirt. By the time he made it back to me, the whites of his eyes showed, and his ears were laid flat against his skull.

Still bracing myself against the tree, I crouched down to stroke his head and back, smoothing the ridge of fur standing upright along his spine. "I don't know how you ended up here, buddy, and I'm sorry I'm asking so much of you, but if it helps at all, I'm awfully glad to have you with me."

Once more showing his uncanny gift for understanding,

Gus chirp-meowed at me and returned to his retrieval efforts. He made three more trips, each time returning with one of the smaller packages, all of which were better behaved than the rucksack had been. His final foray was to the furthest, largest, and least cooperative of the bundles.

I shaded my eyes, though there was no sun in the sky to shade them from, and watched the orange cat tug at the package wedged into the rocks. A cursory examination of the smaller ones had confirmed that they were the herbs, which meant the last remaining one was our food. Our only food.

My stomach grumbled a protest at the thought, and I skimmed my gaze over the desolate mountainside in the vague hope of seeing a way out of this mess. Or perhaps a magical smorgasbord. None appeared, of course, and I returned my attention to Gus in time to see the string snap, sending him tumbling backward.

"Gus!" I yelped. I put an involuntary hand out, as if I could somehow stop him, but the agile cat regained his feet, twitching his fur in irritation, and my hand returned to my side, fingers curled into my palm. The cat started back toward the bundle.

"Leave it," I called. The cat paused to look over his shoulder at me, then back at the package. Briefly—oh, so briefly, because it would have been utter folly—I considered going up the hill to join him. Then I shook my head at myself and at the cat, whose attention was on me again.

"Leave it," I repeated. "It's only food. We'll find something else." My brain skipped around the questions of how and where, because I had no answers. I knew only that I didn't want to figure it out without the cat that Keven had apparently stowed in my rucksack along with the provisions. Blessed, blessed Keven.

As Gus picked his way back down the slope to me, I crouched again and sorted through the packets he had retrieved, my fingers unerringly settling on the ones that contained the heal-all, the comfrey, and the boneset. I hesitated over the latter. Named for what early herbal practitioners thought it good for, Keven had told me, the herb was now used mostly for fevers—unless it was imbued with magick to breathe life into its name. But the gargoyle's warning to me as she'd packed the rucksack still rang grim in my ears.

"The Otherworld is not our world," she'd said. "Your magick ...you mustn't use it. The elements there might not be the same as they are here. There's no way of knowing how they will respond—or if they will at all. Or worse, what you might attract if you try."

I shivered anew at the portent behind her words—and the memory of Bedivere's answering scowl—and shoved the boneset back into the rucksack. The thought of Bedivere had conjured another memory, this one of the shifter lying crumpled and maimed on the cavern floor, his scowl gone at last—forever. And the others likely so as well, despite Jeanne's assurances that she would see them safely out, because how could she have done? A few hexes against the horned god himself? She hadn't stood a chance. None of them had.

I leaned against the tree and let my butt sink back down to the ground, ignoring the bruises and aches and protests. I blinked back the heat of tears and swallowed against the heart lodged in my throat. I'd known they hadn't stood a chance, and yet I'd still left. Left Jeanne. Left the crones and midwitches. Left Natalie...

And landed here. In this—whatever this place was. And now they were dead, and I was as good as, and—

Gus nudged under my hand and then rolled onto his back, stretching all four paws out in a request for a belly rub. I half-laughed, half-sobbed as I complied. The warmth of life beneath my fingers gave me something to focus on in the present and pulled me out of my pity party. I let my touch linger on the cat's softness. I willed myself to feel the contours of his belly and how the short hairs there gave way to the longer ones on his back, and to feel his purr vibrate through my fingertips.

Closing my eyes, I let the sensations fill me, ground me. My breathing slowed and deepened. A weight settled into my core. I would have liked to think of it as determination, but it was too heavy for that. *Resignation,* I thought. *It's resignation.*

Because I couldn't—wouldn't—let the others' sacrifices be for nothing, not without at least trying to find my way to Camlann and Morok—and to Lucan. I owed them all that much ... Crones, midwitches, Bedivere ...

Natalie.

I took a final shuddering breath, then wiped my eyes and nose on the back of my hand, wiped the hand against my already-filthy cloak, and straightened my one good shoulder. Having come this far, I owed *myself* that much.

Now I just needed to decide where to start. I needed water to steep the herbs, but did I dare use my magick to get it?

"Remember what Keven said," my Edie-voice warned me.

I sighed. I was pretty sure I could handle anomalies in how my magick behaved here, but the idea of what it might attract was less appealing. In my current condition, inviting the possibility of attack seemed ill advised at best.

Jaws clenched, I tucked the packets of herbs into the rucksack, hefted myself awkwardly to my feet, and let my gaze follow the steep slope of the mountain down, down, down to the black ribbon below. The more I stared at it, the less like a river it looked, but it was all we had. I pushed aside my misgivings and glanced down at the cat.

"Cross your metaphorical fingers, my friend," I told him. "Because here we go."

With my faithful companion mincing along at my side, I began the long, painstaking—heavy on the pain part of that— trek down the mountainside.

CHAPTER 11

I'D BEEN RIGHT. WHATEVER THE BLACK RIBBON WAS, IT WAS NO river.

I stood at a distance—more like keeping my distance—and eyed the unmoving line that stretched as far as I could see in first one direction, then the other. It sat about a foot off the surface, with thin filaments, also black, attaching it to the ground—although I couldn't tell if they held it down or up. Either way, it wasn't a river.

My parched mouth reminded me of how much I'd hoped for water. I tried to form saliva to relieve the dryness but swallowing only made me wish harder. At my feet, Gus yowled plaintively.

"I know, buddy," I said. "I'm ... working on it."

But was I? With no river at the end of our slow slither down the remaining mountainside and only more of the same desolate landscape—only flatter—now that we were here and no herbal relief on the figurative horizon for my throbbing shoulder and wrist ...

I swallowed again, this time in an effort to keep the stirrings of panic at bay. Fuck, I thought. And then I thought it again. Because fuckity, fuck, fuck, *fuck*. What in the goddess's name was I supposed to do, just pick a direction, any direction, and start walking? I mean, I supposed we could rule out the one we'd just come from, but still.

I let the rucksack slide from my good shoulder onto the ground and picked my way across the rocks to the line. Resting my weight on the staff, I eased my battered body into another crouch and leaned closer to peer at the black strand.

"A ley line, do you think?" my Edie-voice mused. *"An Otherworld version?"*

I shook my head. "Not attached to the ground like that," I said. "It's more …" I put one knee on the ground so I could lean in closer.

"Fibrous," I muttered. I sat back on my heels again. "Almost like a rope, maybe? But how is it being held up like that? No, it has to be solid. More like a—a pipe!"

I almost yelled the last word as hope and realization collided in one glorious surge, and beside me, Gus arched his back and hissed his displeasure at being startled, then gave a low growl in the back of his throat. I ignored his ire and pushed to my feet, aches and pains almost forgotten in my excitement.

"A pipe, Gus! That means we might have water after all. We just need a way to break it."

I cast my gaze around, looking for a heavy-enough rock, but not too heavy, because I only had one usable arm. Maybe a sharp one instead.

"A pipe? To carry water here, in the Otherworld?" my Edie-voice asked.

The question was like a cold dash of the liquid we so badly needed, because she—it—was right. Gods and goddesses were hardly likely to need mechanical things like pipes in a world built on their magick, were they?

"Fuck," I muttered. I closed my eyes and leaned on the staff, swaying on my feet. My head ached fiercely, and my legs shook with the effort of remaining under me. I was on the verge of collapse, and the black ribbon wasn't a river, wasn't a pipe, wasn't a ley line …

Gus continued growling. I hushed him absently, trying to push through my muddled thoughts and the fogginess I was pretty sure came at least in part from dehydrated brain tissue. Dear goddess, I needed water, I thought wearily, but I needed rest, too. The question came down to which one—

Gus.

Gus was growling.

Once again, it belatedly occurred to me that the cat might know more than I did. Then I knew, too, and what little fluid remained in my body turned to ice crystals.

We weren't alone anymore.

THERE WAS NO SUN AND SO THERE COULD BE NO SHADOW, BUT that didn't diminish by a single iota the impression of cold and dark that emanated from the thing looming over us. I felt it even before I opened my eyes and saw it.

A spider.

A gigantic, freaking enormous, massively huge spider about the size of a small house, complete with a heavy round body that was coated in fine hairs and supported on long, segmented legs—eight of them—and ... and ...

And there the spider idea floundered, because the head—

The head was human. Or god, maybe, given where we stood. Or where I hoped we stood. But with the long gray hair surrounding a lined, weathered face held up by a neck atop shoulders that sprouted arms instead of palps, it most definitely was not spider. Except for maybe—

Oh dear goddess, its eyes—her eyes? Freaking hell, *the* eyes —all eight of them—were round and brown and jewel-like, like tourmalines, and lined up in rows with two dominant ones topped by two smaller above them and a row of four below and—

The eight legs each took a step closer to us, and I almost choked on the shriek I swallowed. It might not be all spider, perhaps, but it was spider enough.

I pinned my staff between my body and my right forearm and bent down to scoop up Gus with my other. Squishing him against my side, I angled my body to keep myself between him and—

The massive creature lowered its body until it rested on the ground, legs folded on either side. The weathered human face gazed down at me with its eight jeweled eyes. A small smile played around lips thinned by age, but no age that was within my grasp. My mind let go of its terror and edged toward awe, for the face studying me was ... ancient. Ageless. I could see it in the timeworn lines of the face—a woman's face—and in the knowing of her half-smile, and in the sorrow and joy and sadness and ... life ... that stared back at me.

Gus wriggled in my grasp, and I let him slide down my hip and onto the ground again. There was no threat here. Not from—

"Who ...?" I let my voice trail off. Was it rude to ask?

"Weaver," she replied. "I am Weaver."

Her words rolled over me and out across the lifeless land, and then back to me again, and tears sprang to my eyes at the sound of them. At the sound of her voice. It was at once a whisper, a roll of thunder, and the most beautiful melody I'd ever heard in my life, stirring in me an ache that was as ageless as the being to whom it belonged.

"And you ..." Weaver—not just Weaver, but *the* Weaver, I was certain—continued to study me. "You are the Morrigan but not the Morrigan."

"I—" My voice cracked on the attempt to speak, and I inhaled deeply. Raggedly.

"You are human, too." Weaver observed, tipping her head to one side. "But not."

I tried again. "It's—a long story," I croaked.

She nodded thoughtfully, her eight gazes lingering on my face. "I can see that. And you are injured."

I blinked down at my arm, which gave an accusatory twinge as if annoyed at having been forgotten. "Yes," I said, moving the staff back into the grip of my left hand. "I fell. When I came through. Up there." I pointed up the mountain for good measure. *Wow, Claire, eloquent.*

The Weaver followed my finger. Her top row of eyes twitched together in a slight frown. "There." She looked back at me. "Through the doorway."

She knew about—?

"I made it," she said dryly, reading my thoughts. "This world. Your world. All the worlds beyond, and the ones beyond those. It is what I do. I spin and I weave, and worlds are born and there are doorways where my webs connect them."

I tried not to think too hard about the multiple doors into multiple worlds concept. I was here for one door only, I reminded myself. Best to keep it simple for sanity's sake.

The Weaver folded her arms across the round bulge of her torso and tapped a thoughtful finger against her lips. "You are one of them," she said. "One of the Destroyers."

"I'm—wait, one what?" I jerked my head back, startled, then shook it, denying her words. Afraid of the consequences they might hold. "You're wrong. I'm not a destroyer of anything."

Unless you counted the three Mages I'd killed. Or the wards I'd accidentally decimated. Or the friends—

I stopped my thoughts there, unwilling to follow them further. Not daring to, lest the ache that resided in my chest should swallow me whole.

"I'm not a destroyer," I reiterated with less adamance than I would have liked. "At least, not on purpose."

"But you are," the Weaver said sadly. "Perhaps through no fault of your own, but you are, nonetheless." She folded her hands before her and lifted a leg from the ground, waving it in a wide circle that encompassed the mountain and the seemingly endless barren land on which we stood.

I followed the motion but frowned. "I don't understand."

"Of course not. You had no way of knowing, and the one who should have told you did not." She shook her head in a gesture as sad as her voice. Then she smiled a soft half-smile.

"But come, my home is not far, and you need care. We will talk later."

Caution made me hesitate. The line from a childhood poem drifted across my mind: *"Will you walk into my parlor?" said the Spider to the Fly.*

It didn't help in the least.

Neither did my Edie-voice's whisper of *"buzz buzz buzz."*

"Very funny," I muttered, and the memory of her voice cackled. But hesitant or not, it wasn't like I had much choice. I wasn't just injured, I was hopelessly lost, had neither food nor water, and—

Gus pressed against my calf and meowed, then minced over to wind himself against one of the Weaver's legs.

And if the cat who had followed me across a barrier between worlds had decided that this was okay, who was I to argue? I retrieved my rucksack from the ground and nodded. "Thank you," I said, by way of agreement.

With much maneuvering on the Weaver's part—because my arm wouldn't let me do it myself—she managed to lift me up to sit in the valley between her head and abdomen, the latter part twitching as Gus climbed up one of her legs to join me.

"Your friend has sharp feet," she remarked.

"Yes." I pried claws from my thigh where the cat clung and sat him atop the rucksack I'd tucked before me. He settled into a loaf and began purring.

The Weaver's head swiveled around, and she stared at the rumbling cat. "It vibrates?"

I couldn't help but smile. "It's called purring. It means he's happy and comfortable."

"Hm." She watched him for a moment, and then nodded. "This pleases me. Now, hold onto my hair so that you do not fall. It will not hurt me."

I did as I was told with my one good arm and then wished I had the use of the other, too, as we took off across the barren land at an eight-legged speed that made me gasp. At first, I jostled up and down, which wasn't comfortable for either one of us, I imagined, but after a few moments I found the rhythm of her stride and settled into it as best I could, given the beating I'd take from the mountain.

Before I knew it, wasteland gave way to the sudden, verdant green of cool forest where trees soared higher than the eye could see—giant cedars like the ones that grew in the rainforest along Canada's west coast. But there were more of them, and they were taller and twice the girth, and—I clutched at the handful of the Weaver's hair I held as she stopped without warning and I almost slid off.

"We are here," she said.

I regained my balance and then looked up ... and up ... and up. And then I gaped in awe at what she called home.

CHAPTER 12

IF IT HAD BEEN HARD TO MAINTAIN MY SEAT AS WE TRAVELED over flat ground, keeping it as we traveled perpendicular to that ground was all but impossible. Especially when I craned my neck this way and that, taking in the intricate marvel that we climbed. Every pattern I had ever seen in nature or woven by the most talented artists on Earth was here, along with others that had not yet been dreamed of. A tapestry spun together in columns and walls, spirals and whorls and waves, in every color of every rainbow that had ever existed. It was beautiful. It was magnificent. It was humbling beyond words.

When the Weaver stopped climbing and her body leveled out again, we were in a vaulted chamber made of the same weavings, these ones iridescent like mother of pearl. Their patterns radiated in every direction possible, seemingly without end, and slow understanding dawned.

"It's the center," I murmured, my voice oddly muffled. "Your home. It's the center of everything."

"It is All," the Weaver agreed, lowering her body to the cavern floor.

Obligingly, I stopped gaping long enough to slide from her back. The surface gave way beneath my weight like a floor made of marshmallow might, and my feet sank past my ankles. I barely noticed, too busy staring at the lace of its structure.

"What do you need?" the Weaver asked. Her voice was muffled by the acoustics of the chamber as mine had been, as if we spoke in a room filled with cotton.

"What? I mean, pardon?" I wrenched my attention from the floor back to her, noticing that Gus, ever the shoulder-cat, had elected to remain atop her, draped between her body and head. I hoped he remembered to keep his claws retracted.

"To heal yourself." She pointed at my arm. "What do you need?"

"Oh." I looked down at myself and sighed at the unmistakable black bruising that had surfaced on the forearm above the wrist. I'd hoped for a sprain rather than a fracture, but that? That didn't look good. *Magick*, I thought. *I need magick.*

"Water," I said instead. "To mix my herbs. And something to wrap around my arm, if you have it."

The Weaver moved away to one of the walls and parted the filaments there. She plucked some of them out and formed them into a bowl and draped others as strands over one arm. She returned to me and handed over the bowl.

"You will have to fill it," she said. "I have no need of water and so no means of collection."

I stared at the empty bowl, my wrist throbbing but Keven's warning ringing again in my head. "I—"

"You have the Morrigan's magick, do you not?"

"Yes, but—can I use it? Here, I mean?" I waved the bowl at the cavern that was the center, as the Weaver had said, of All.

"Here, yes." She nodded. "Here, you are protected from detection. Out there, I would not advise it."

Detection? From what? I opened my mouth to ask, but my tongue had cleaved to my palate from lack of fluid, and I decided there would be time for my questions—so many of them—after I'd dealt with more pressing matters. I hobbled across the marshmallow floor to the wall and leaned my staff against it, waiting to be sure it wouldn't disappear into the filamented depths. The staff stayed put, and I turned my attention to the task of conjuring water.

But where to even begin? In my own world, I could connect to the elements of Air, Earth, Fire, and Water. Did those same elements exist in the Otherworld? I supposed there was only one way to find out—hopefully without any of the unexpected consequences Keven had muttered about. With a last, less-than-convinced glance at the Weaver, I closed my eyes.

In the time since my battle with Morok, I had spent countless hours perfecting my control over the power the Morrigan had allowed me to keep. Not in the first couple of weeks after our return to the Earth house, perhaps. Those had been spent in utter disbelief. Paralyzing grief. Soul-deep denial. But as I had processed the events and come to grips with them, I had slowly determined that I never again wanted to be unable to call on the magick I had been given. I might still consider it more of a curse than a blessing—because it was—but it was mine, nonetheless, and I was determined to master it.

Bedivere had been the only one to know about my practice. He had accompanied me on my forays into the woods and stood silent guard while I alternately wrestled with my confidence, my belief, my will. He'd never said a word about it to me, but the weight of his expectations had helped to drive me, helped me to stay focused on my ultimate goal: that of rescuing his brother.

I focused on that again now. On my reason for being here, on the thought of Lucan, on the memory of the sacrifice Bedivere had made to get me this far. I focused, and I reached for Water, and …

"Huh," said the Weaver.

My eyes popped open, and I followed the gaze of her many eyes toward the ceiling. Stalactites had formed above me and were dripping water into the chamber, each drop falling soundlessly to the floor.

"Huh," I echoed the Weaver. "I didn't think—I wasn't sure—"

"Frankly, neither was I," she said, her appraising gaze running over me. She took the bowl from me and moved it under the stalactites, catching the drops as they fell. When the bowl was full, she returned it to me. "You can turn it off now."

I turned inward again and found the connection, then pulled my will back from it. The connection resisted. I reassembled my thoughts and tugged again, but Water was unyielding. Rigid. Locked onto me as if—

A hand settled on my shoulder and the connection dissolved as it should. I let out a shaky breath. That had been ...

"Weird as fuck?" my Edie-voice suggested.

I caught back a laugh born of exhaustion, pain, and the beginnings of hysteria. Which would also explain the Water element's weird resistance, when I thought about it. My control of magick was bound to be a little wonky after the events of the day. Once I'd looked after my arm and had some sleep, I'd be fine again. Right as rain, as my grandmother would have said. Tickety-boo. Just peach—

"You are ill?" the Weaver inquired.

"No." I shook my head and would have toppled but for her hand still on my shoulder. "No, I'm just tired, I think. Thank you for your help letting go of the Water."

She shrugged. "I do what needs to be done. What now?"

"Now I do what needs to be done, too."

I STAYED WITH THE WEAVER FOR TWO DAYS. OR WHAT PASSED for days, because again, no sun, and on the opposite side of the spectrum, no dark, either. The world here, the Otherworld, seemed to exist in a perpetual state of daylight that had no actual light source.

The Weaver herself had wrapped my arm when it had become obvious that I couldn't. After some probing and swearing, I discovered the fracture site in the forearm itself, thankfully, and not the wrist joint. Jeanne had once told me how many bones made up the wrist. I couldn't remember the number offhand, but it was a lot, and it often meant that a break to the joint took longer to heal than one to a straight bone. I didn't have that kind of time.

I didn't have *any* time, but neither did I have much choice. The Weaver's warning—added to Keven's—about not using my magick in the Otherworld meant that I would have only my staff for defense, and that meant I needed both my arms. So I counted my stay in sleeps, pulled water from the stalactites, mixed my herbs, and imbued them with all the healing magick I could muster as I tried not to think about how long it took bones to heal.

But something about being in the Otherworld must have made my magick stronger, its healing more potent, because when I woke on the third "morning" of my stay, the pain in my arm was gone.

"It is the ambrosia," the Weaver said, placing a dollop of gelatinous, bright blue goop into one of the bowls she'd made for me from her filament. The same gelatinous, bright blue goop that she'd been feeding me for breakfast, lunch, and dinner since my arrival.

"Pardon?" I looked up from unwinding more of the same filament from around my arm.

"The ambrosia," she repeated, pointing at the bowl. "It is the food of all the gods here. I think it must be feeding the Morrigan part of you."

I held my unwrapped arm up and twisted it this way and that. There wasn't the slightest twinge of discomfort in it. The arm felt fine, the rest of my poor, battered body felt fine, *I* felt fine. Better than I had in weeks, in fact, if not years. Did all the gods and goddesses feel this good?

I eyed the goop I'd been reluctantly consuming so far, my feelings mixed. In light of the Weaver's observation, I had a new appreciation for it, yes, but as a long-term substitute for nutrition, I wasn't sure I could get past the slimy texture. Or the fact that it smelled—and tasted—like rotted vegetation. I hoped it tasted better to the gods for whom it was the only sustenance.

The Weaver pushed the bowl closer to me. "Eat," she said. "You will leave after. I will take you to the path you seek."

It was the first time she'd offered, and my heart gave a hopeful little skip. She'd closed her many spider eyes and drifted off to sleep when I'd tried to tell her my reason for being in the Otherworld on my first day here. On the second day, she'd simply turned and left the chamber when I'd broached the topic again and mentioned Camlann.

In short, she'd made it patently clear that she put up with my presence on sufferance and had no interest in me beyond that. She had offered no help other than sheltering and feeding me. Given her indifference—and who she was—I hadn't worked up the nerve to ask any more questions, no matter how much answers might have helped.

"Thank you," I said. "I know you don't like what I'm doing—"

"I neither like nor dislike," she replied, resting back on her spider haunches. She shrugged the human shoulders that supported her head and held her arms. "I make. That is all I do. The worlds that are born and the lives that spawn from them are not my concern. I will show you the path to this Camlann you seek, and you will succeed in your quest or not. That is not my concern, either."

It was on the tip of my tongue to ask why she would do even that much, if she didn't care, but a wiser part of me scooped up some rotted vegetation ambrosia and gagged it down before I could. If the Weaver of All wanted to show me the path, I wasn't going to say anything that might make her change her mind.

CHAPTER 13

I WASN'T, HOWEVER, WILLING TO GIVE UP ALTOGETHER. AS WE walked side by side through the forest after my next sleep, I made another attempt at getting information. If nothing else, the Weaver was less likely to walk away from me here, I reasoned, so it was worth a try.

I cleared my throat, and the spider beside me looked down. I tried not to dwell on the part about walking through the woods beside a spider in the first place. Or about having stayed in the home of one for the last two days.

"You called me a Destroyer on the day you found me," I said. "Why?"

She turned her head and eight tourmaline eyes to the front again, and I listened to the staccato thuds of her feet hitting the ground in succession as we walked. Her silence stretched so long that I thought she would again not answer, but at last she spoke. "You remember where I found you? Where you entered through the door?"

"Of course."

"The mountain there did not always look like that. Once, it lived and gave life and looked much like this, but then the ether bled through and took that life."

The ether? I remembered Lucan mentioning it once, a lifetime ago, it seemed, when I'd asked about the shades. The Between, he'd called it. I said as much to the Weaver.

"It is as good a name as any, I suppose," she agreed. "It is what exists between the All. Between everything."

I tried—and failed—to bend my mind around the explanation. "I don't understand."

"It simply is," she said with a shrug of her human shoulders. "As I am. I make. It unmakes."

I thought it over, but nope. I still wasn't getting it. I shook my head to let her know, and she pointed with one hand at the forest we walked through, her gesture encompassing.

"Tell me what you see."

"Trees," I said, hoping I didn't sound obtuse. "Underbrush. The ground. A path."

"And between them?"

I frowned. "Air, I suppose, although I can't technically see that."

"And what do you see in the air?"

"I—" I shrugged. "I have no idea."

"Ether." The Weaver reached up and plucked a needle from a conifer branch above her head. She stopped walking and held it out to me. "Or the Between, as you call it. It is in this needle, too. And in the cat that sits on me"—she patted Gus, who rode behind her head—"and in the sack you carry, and in you. It is a part of everything I make, between the wholes, between the pieces, between what makes the pieces."

I stared at the needle in her palm—pine, I thought—and then at the world around me, trying to understand. A distant part of my brain stirred and dusted itself off. Somewhere in it, I thought I might know what she was talking about, but the harder I tried to grasp the idea, the deeper it burrowed in its efforts to elude me. I sighed. So did the Weaver.

She started walking again with the staccato *thud-thud-thud-thud, thud-thud-thud-thud*, and I trotted to keep up.

"What about the Destroyer thing?" I asked. Perhaps if she explained that, the rest would make sense, too. "Why am I one?"

"You tear apart the world that birthed you, do you not?"

Tear apart—

My breath caught on a sudden flash of insight. Of course. The splinters. She was talking about the splinters—and by extrapolation, she meant that the Crones were the destroyers. I sped up my steps until I could cut in front of her, then I stopped. The Weaver did likewise, gazing down at me without expression, as if she already knew what I was going to say.

I said it anyway. "We have no choice," I began. "We needed to create the splinters to keep Morok—"

But once again she cut off my attempts to explain.

"Reasons change nothing," she said. "When you tear apart, you release the Between, and the Between devours All. It does not care about your why, it only does what it has always done."

I was silent for a long moment, absorbing her words, chasing again—and still unsuccessfully—the knowledge that teased along the edges of my brain. Another question occurred to me.

"Did the Morrigan know?" I asked. "Did she understand what would happen if we split the world?"

"Perhaps. Perhaps not. It does not matter any more than your reasons matter. If she had let Morok go unchecked, he would simply have caused the destruction himself." She paused, her expression thoughtful, and then corrected herself, "No, not caused. Hastened. Because the end of All is inevitable."

So she did know about Morok, I thought, but her other words seemed just a little more important. I drew my head back as unease slithered across my shoulders.

"Inevitable?" I echoed. "What do you mean inevitable? Why? And how?"

The Weaver moved forward again, and I ducked as she passed over me and the hairs on her abdomen scraped my head. "The unmaking is greater than the making," she said. "It always has been. It cannot be stopped. Not even here. Not even by me."

Again, I scurried to catch up. "Wait, what unmaking? And why can't you—" I skidded to a stop, remembering the barren landscape I'd arrived in. The lack of water, color, movement ... the lack of life.

"The place where I came through," I murmured.

"Yes," she agreed. "When one of those that your kind has placed here ceases to be, they leave their lands unprotected. When you release the ether with your destruction, it removes all but the skeleton of what was their place in this world."

My last, tiny hope of having things make sense sputtered out. Those my kind had placed here? What in holy freaking hell did *that* mean? Was I a Destroyer of that, too? Plodding rather than trotting behind the Weaver now, I scrubbed both hands over my face, torn between asking and simply giving up before my brain short-circuited. Before I could reach a decision, I collided with a hairy spider leg and staggered back. The Weaver had stopped.

"That is the path that will take you to Camlann," she said, pointing into the distance to where a strand of spider web disappeared, perpendicular to the one we'd been following. She looked down at me as I drew abreast of her. "You must not let it out of your sight. Do not follow any other path that leads from it. If you do, you will be lost forever. There are other beings here who will not care to help a lesser one than they, and I will not return for you. You understand?"

Her instructions were simple—and sobering—and I nodded. But a shiver ran down my spine as my gaze traveled the vast prairie stretching before me, just beyond the edge of the forest we'd come through. The spider strand, black like the one we'd followed and the others we'd passed on our way here, ran through the middle of it in an unswerving line seemingly forever.

"That," observed my Edie-voice, *"is a helluva long walk."*

It wasn't wrong. How many days would it take me to cross a grassland of that immensity? Was Camlann at the edge of it, or was it even further?

"How far?" I asked, turning back to the Weaver. "To Camlann, I—"

The word *mean* died on my lips. The Weaver was gone.

Where she had been standing, Gus sat watching me, and a new strand of web stretched upward from the one we'd followed here. Like the others, there was no end in sight. And no sign of the Weaver of All. She'd disappeared. Gone back to what she did. I stared up for another few seconds, squinting my eyes as I searched the endless, unchanging gray sky, then I turned back to Gus.

"Well, my friend, it looks like it's just us again. You ready?"

With a *prrt* in reply, the cat set out alongside the strand, his tail high and kinked at the tip. I adjusted the rucksack strap across my shoulder and started after him—then stopped again as the oh-so-elusive memory I'd searched for earlier finally surfaced in my brain. A tidbit gleaned from a science documentary I'd watched long ago.

Because that was what the Weaver's mention of the ether —the Between—had reminded me of. Science. More specifically, dark energy, the stuff of quantum physics that made up well over half the universe. The stuff that astronomers theorized was slowly expanding and becoming stronger and would eventually result in the destruction of the universe itself.

Or, if the Weaver was right, unmake it. And we Crones had been helping it all along, and if Morok succeeded in regaining his powers ...

I almost quit right then and there. Having to stop Morok in order to save the world—*my* world—had been bad enough. But this? Being responsible for stopping the destruction of the very universe itself? Or at least slowing it, if the Weaver was right about the inevitable part? There was just so much *nope* in that idea that I didn't know where to start.

Except what else was there to do? Turn around and go home? Even if by some miracle I found my way back to the door between here and Earth, Morok would still come for me —assuming Cernunnos didn't get me on my way through first —and I would still fight him, and I would still do it alone, because the others ...

Ever-present grief thickened my throat. I closed my eyes and clenched my jaw and waited for it to pass, then let out the long, shaky breath I'd been holding as I made myself finish the thought. Because the others were gone. And I was all that was left. And ...

I stared after Gus, who had become a faint ripple through the prairie grass that had swallowed him, raised tail and all. A burble of laughter welled up from a place in me that was arguably not entirely sane anymore.

"And if nothing else," I told the Otherworld, "I might still be able to save the cat."

At least for a little while.

CHAPTER 14

WE WALKED FOR THREE SLEEPS, GUS AND I, NEVER STEPPING out of sight of the spider silk we followed. The Weaver had given me a sac filled with ambrosia and another that I had filled with water, but even though we had used both sparingly —Gus turning his nose up at the former but grateful for the latter—the rucksack across my shoulder had become ominously light. And there was still no end, and no Camlann, in sight.

When I got too tired to push through the endless prairie grass, I would trample down a circle big enough to lie in, and we would rest as well as we could. *Well* being a subjective word, given the needles of grass that poked through clothes and skin alike. Not even my cloak provided any protection, with its many holes and tears and its magick long since gone. I briefly debated leaving it behind but, like the staff, it provided a connection to my past that I wasn't willing to give up. So, instead, I folded it into a bed for Gus. The cat might have to go hungry, but at least he could sleep in comfort.

At last, on our fourth day of travel, we had a breakthrough. Literally.

Gus had given up leading the way in favor of following the easier path that I forged, so I was the first to hit the wall. Not a solid wall, exactly, although enough so that colliding with it knocked me onto my butt beside the cat. It was more … rubbery. And it was translucent, letting in enough light from the other side that, if I peered closely, I could make out towering mountains, blue skies, a ribbon of what looked to be water—actual, real water this time—and the continuation of the spider strand.

I sat, supporting myself on my hands, and regarded both

81

landscape and unexpected barrier, neither of which I had seen coming. And no wonder. If I leaned just a few inches back, both seemed to disappear, leaving what looked like an extension of the flat, desolate landscape we had been traveling all along. Like a reflection, but without me and Gus in it.

When I leaned forward, however ...

I caught my breath as details shimmered into focus. The ribbon of water became a narrow waterfall, cascading from an impossible height between two mountain peaks to become a river that flowed unbending toward me, lined on either side by towering pine trees. Trees and river alike ended abruptly at the translucent wall. And the silk strand we'd been following? That ran down the center of the river, straight back toward the waterfall.

"You have *got* to be kidding," I muttered.

I shifted as far as I could to the left without moving my butt. The other side of the barrier disappeared, and the wall became the reflection again, solid to the touch when I reached for it. When I moved to the right, the same thing happened. But as soon as I centered myself on the river, everything came back into focus.

I picked up my staff from where it had fallen, climbed to my feet, braced myself, and reached forward with my other hand. It went easily through the wall and into the spray of water from where the river crashed around a rock, and it returned wet when I pulled it back.

"Fuck," I muttered. I thought about the Weaver's warning not to stray from the strand and repeated with a little more vehemence and lot more dismay, "*Fuck.*"

Because I wasn't going to have much choice in this, was I? I was about to get wet. Very wet.

"*Fuckity fuck,*" my Edie-voice agreed. I wasn't imagining her as often as I used to, I realized. The thought sent a pang through me. I wasn't ready to let go of the memory, but neither did I have time to think about her the way I once did

—or for the conversations I liked to carry on with her. I'd have to try harder.

But first, I had to get through the wall and not drown.

My preparations were minimal. I slipped off the rucksack and set it on the ground, then undid the clasp of my cloak. The poor thing could have used a good dunking to freshen it up, but I didn't know how deep the water would be when we went through the barrier, and I couldn't chance having the fabric wrap around my legs and weigh me down. I shoved it into the rucksack beside the pouches the Weaver had given me, then arranged it into a hollow.

It wasn't a bad thing after all that our supplies had run low at this point after all, I thought as I scooped up Gus. At least it gave me more room for other things. Important things. I stuffed the cat into the hollow of the cloak.

"It's temporary," I promised, doing up the buckle before he recovered from his surprise. Cats were excellent swimmers, but I didn't want to risk getting separated from him in the river, not with so many unknowables waiting for us.

Ignoring his howls of complaints from the bag, I picked up the staff again, slung the rucksack over my shoulder, hoped the water wouldn't be too deep, and pushed my body into the gelatinous wall.

Instantly, memories of another like it flooded my brain and panic threatened. I sucked in a breath and got goo instead of air. As before, it filled my mouth, my nostrils, my eyes. I gagged, and my panic leveled up. I held myself rigid for a second. *Stop*, I commanded my brain. *We did this before, and we can do it again. Just focus.*

I counted to three, then tugged my hand up from my side and scooped the gelatin away from my face. I took a breath, and then, remembering, I pushed one foot forward, dragged the other to join it, and forced my torso forward to follow, and—

All resistance disappeared. With no time—or way—to

stop myself, I plunged headfirst into the churning rapids. I inhaled a shocked breath, icy water closed over my head, and I sank like a stone, taking Gus with me.

Apparently not all of the Weaver's walls were created the same.

CHAPTER 15

I FOUGHT MY WAY TO THE SURFACE, GAGGING AND COUGHING up the water I'd inhaled. The river roiled around me, its waters fast and ferocious, carrying me away from the wall with dizzying speed and slamming me into one hidden boulder after another. Again and again, I went under. Again and again, I surfaced and sucked for air. Again and again, I tried desperately to tear the rucksack strap from my shoulder so that I could lift Gus, too, above the water.

When I was able to open my eyes against the rush and see through the foam, I caught glimpses of the spider strand stretching above me, but I couldn't fling myself high enough to reach it. Another boulder slammed into me—or I into it— did it even matter?—and I grimly turned my attention to keeping my head from becoming the point of impact. Another broken arm, I could endure. A fractured skull? Maybe not so much.

Eventually, an eon later, the river brought me close enough to the shore that I could pull myself out of the water. I lay face down on the riverbank for long minutes, exhausted and gasping, the current still tugging at my feet. The rucksack shifted against my back, and, dimly, I remembered the cat I'd stuffed inside it.

I gritted my teeth, pushed up on shaking arms, collapsed, tried again. On hands and knees, I crawled further up the shore, leaving the river and the spider strand behind, relieved to be away from the former and too freaking tired to care about the latter. The rucksack moved again and Gus's howls rose above the water's roar. I sagged sideways and onto my butt on the rocks, then slid the wet strap over my head. The rucksack dropped to the ground and then thrashed about as I tried to undo its buckle.

"Damn it, Gus, you're not helping," I growled over the roar of the river. "Hold still."

He didn't, but I managed to get it open in spite of him, and the soaked, bedraggled, and highly indignant cat bolted from the interior, staggering about as he tried to shake water from all four feet at once. Amusement bubbled in my chest, but I was too tired to smile. Leaving Gus to attempt drying himself with his long pink tongue, I lay back, oblivious to the stones digging into my shoulder blades, and covered my eyes with one forearm.

For the second time in the space of a few days, I assessed the damage inflicted on my body. Everything felt bruised and battered again, and I was pretty sure I would be multicolored from head to toe in a few hours, but—again for the second time—I was still alive. I just wasn't sure how reassuring that was anymore.

Or how much more of this I could take.

I thought about sitting up to take stock of our situation, but my body refused to cooperate, and surely it deserved a reprieve after what it had just survived. And besides, the sun felt so, *so* good on my—

I lifted my arm and blinked up at the sky, shielding my eyes against the glare. Sun. There was sun. Warm, golden, healing ... oh dear goddess, I'd had no idea how much I'd missed the feel of it. I closed my eyes again and lay for long, luxurious minutes simply soaking it in, wishing I could sink into the sleep that tugged at me. Longing to do so.

Unfortunately, my brain was less interested in the idea of rest than my body was.

We should get moving, it nudged. *You don't know how much further it is. It might be just behind that waterfall—like the door was in Confluence. And you'll be less sore if you move, too. If you lie here—*

"Oh, for fuck's sake," I muttered. My words were lost in

the unending thunder of water, however. Giving in, I levered myself up onto my elbows. Gus looked up briefly, then returned to his grooming. I reached for the rucksack and pulled the cloak from it. I didn't need it with the sun's warmth, but it would dry faster if I wore it—and so would the canvas of the rucksack itself.

I set the cloak aside and dug further into the sack, withdrawing two ruptured and deflated sacs, remnants of what the Weaver had given me. The water one was no great loss with the river flowing beside us, but the ambrosia one …

"Shit," I muttered as my stomach grumbled. I tossed both sacs aside and continued my excavation of the rucksack. Keven's herb packets were still intact—albeit soggy—but of little use at the moment without a vessel for water to soak them in. I grimaced and put the packets away again. My bruised body would have to fend for itself this time around.

I heaved myself to my feet and frowned. It felt like I was missing something, but—

Loss buried itself like a fist in my gut. My staff. Where was—

My gaze settled on a long stick protruding from between two boulders near the river's edge, and I almost cried from sheer relief. Sniffling, I grabbed up the discarded cloak and half-walked, half-slithered across the loose stones of the shoreline to retrieve the stick. Setting one end against the ground, I closed my eyes and leaned my forehead against the familiar wood. I didn't know how I'd managed to hang onto it in the water, but I had, and my gratitude knew no bounds. In the midst of so much loss, I was glad to at least have this much.

A smile played over my lips as Gus, who had finished his drying session, wound around my ankles.

"And you," I agreed, opening my eyes to look down at him. "I still have you."

We followed the river—and the spider strand above it—toward the waterfall that was now much closer thanks to the river carrying us as far as it had. A blessing in painful disguise, I supposed. We might even make it there before we stopped for the night. I grinned. And we might even have an actual night, now that we had sun. What a concept.

Behind my lightheartedness, however, the feeling of missing something nagged at me, becoming more irritating with every step. I picked my way over and between rocks in the wake of the more agile cat leading the way, mulling over what might be wrong. I had everything with me that I'd brought—staff, rucksack, cloak, cat—and yes, I'd lost the ambrosia, but that wasn't it. *It* wasn't something concrete. It was more like a thought I couldn't quite—wait.

My steps slowed. Stopped. I looked sideways at the river. At the current flowing not from the waterfall, but toward it. Except that was impossible. Water didn't work that way. *Physics* didn't work that way. Unless …

Suddenly my ears tuned in to the roar of the water that I'd been listening to all along but not hearing, not understanding. A roar that had been too loud to be the river and too close to be the waterfall. I lifted my gaze from the river to the cascade, then dropped it to where the two should meet … but didn't.

My heart sank to my toes. My stomach joined it. I moved forward again, shaking my head in time with each step I took. Ten feet. Twenty. Fifty.

The thunderous roar grew ever louder, drowning out even my thoughts, and then—there it was.

A chasm wider than the river that flowed into it on one side or the waterfall that flowed into it on the other cut across both, so deep that I couldn't see the bottom, if there was one. So long that I couldn't see an end in either direction. And there, stretched across it from river to waterfall and disappearing into the latter, was the spider strand.

"Fuck," I said.

CHAPTER 16

IT WAS GUS WHO CAME UP WITH THE SOLUTION TO OUR chasm-crossing problem— although *solution* was an awfully loose term for his idea of using the spider silk as a balance beam.

Because, yes, it meant that we would be following the strand as the Weaver had instructed and, yes, the strand did cross the chasm and, yes, it might even be thick enough to support our weight—well, at least the cat's—but that didn't stop utter horror from turning my blood to ice when I saw him nonchalantly sauntering along it.

"Gus!" I yelled. I clapped a hand over my mouth as it occurred to me, too late, that my voice might startle him and cause him to fall into depths too dark for my eyes to penetrate. Sure enough, the ginger cat stopped halfway between river and waterfall and looked back over his shoulder. A panicky part of me wanted him to turn around and make his way back, but how? The strand was wide enough to accommodate one-way travel, perhaps, but a turn? Even for the sure-footed feline, that seemed unlikely.

My thoughts tumbled together in a maelstrom. Had we taken a wrong turn somewhere? Strayed away from the original strand the Weaver had shown me? Dear goddess, had she deliberately sent us on an impossible path, wanting us to fail despite her claims of impartiality?

Halfway across the chasm, Gus sat down, tail curled around him, and began washing a paw without seeming to notice—or care about—his precarious position. I swallowed a lump the size of my heart, plenty terrified for both of us.

Gus stood again and returned to his trek, growing smaller with every step as I watched helplessly from my side of the chasm. And then the cat disappeared through a gap in the curtain of waterfall and there was only me and—

"Jesus Christ on a cracker and fuckity fuck and fucking *hell*," I muttered under my breath as I snatched up the rucksack, stuffed my head through the strap, and marched toward the spider strand. If this was the only way to Morok, then this was the way I would go.

Because if the Weaver was right, and this entire situation —the whole, rotten, disastrous mess—was at least in part due to the Morrigan and the Crones, me included, I had to see it through.

I hoisted my cloak up around my thighs, took a deep breath, and stepped up onto the spider strand.

WITH THE RUCKSACK AT MY BACK, I INCHED ALONG THE SILK, carrying the staff horizontally for balance. I dreaded looking down, but the strand was the width of a street curb, and I had no choice but to watch my feet, putting one carefully in front of the other, trying not to see what lay—or, rather, didn't lay —below them.

Bravado carried me about a third of the way across. Determination carried me to the halfway point. Sheer pigheadedness got me to the three-quarter mark. I was a mere twenty feet away now, and the waterfall's spray had soaked my cloak and skin again, but I didn't look up. I didn't dare. Not yet.

One step, another, another. The thunder of the falls enveloped me and vibrated through the silk beneath my feet. Then, at the top periphery of my vision, I saw the curtain of water. The gap into which Gus had disappeared. I'd done it. I'd reached the other—

My trailing foot slipped, and I pitched forward. The staff

flew from my grip as my arms pinwheeled wildly, and I watched in slow-motion horror as it tumbled end over end into the waterfall. But I had no time to mourn its loss. No time to do anything more than grab for the silk strand as I fell full length on top of it, grunting as all the air left my lungs on impact and my diaphragm spasmed.

When I was a child, we'd called it having the wind knocked out of us. It had been a terrifying experience then, not being able to drag oxygen back into our bodies. It was no less so now. My diaphragm went rigid against the silk strand I lay on, and I fought the urge to sit up to relieve it. I didn't know how I'd managed to wrap my arms around the strand—how I hadn't plunged headfirst into the abyss—but I had, and there was no way in hell I was letting go until I'd recovered my breath and could trust the rest of me to function, too.

Slowly, the spasm in my midsection eased, air returned to my lungs, and my heart stopped trying to fight its way out of my ribcage. Even more slowly, I opened my eyes and raised my head to view my surroundings. Well, some of them. Because, looking down? Not happening.

I focused instead on what lay before me. The silk strand, wet with spray from the waterfall, disappeared through the gap in the curtain of water that Gus had walked into. A gap that lay just a few feet away.

You can do this, my inner voice assured me. *It's just four feet, five at the most. You don't even have to stand up. You can just slither on your belly.*

I considered the words and decided the voice was right—it was odd that it didn't sound like the usual Edie one, but it was still right. If I just loosened my hold on the strand and moved my hands forward ...

If I loosened my hold on the strand ...

If I loosened ...

I tilted my head to the left and frowned at the arm that had fused to the silk.

"Four feet," I told it, but my words were lost in the roar of water dropping into the chasm beneath, and my limb gave no indication that it heard.

"Please?" I yelled. "We really have no choice, you know. We can't stay here forever."

The arm twitched. The movement transferred down it to my forearm, my wrist, my fingers. Fraction by cramped fraction, the latter let go their hold on the strand. I slid them ahead, gripped tight again, and hauled myself a tiny bit forward. Then I repeated the process.

It took forever—just like this whole ill-fated trek into the Otherworld was taking forever—and I was so focused on my task that I let out a muffled shriek and almost fell off when a cold nose touched mine. I pulled my head back as far as I could force it and stared at the orange cat in the shadows before me. Gus blinked back lazily, then leapt sideways off the strand. I shrieked again and grabbed for him, then grabbed for my anchor, then stopped grabbing—and moving—and breathing. Astonishment settled over me, then relief, then sheer, unadulterated triumph as I looked down at the solid rock beneath the spider strand.

I'd done it. I'd made it. For real this time. I had, in fact, been crawling along that damned strand over terra firma (or whatever it was called in the god world) for a good ten feet. I squeezed my eyes shut and rested my chin on the spider silk, letting my elation wash over me.

I'd done it, I thought again. I'd crossed the chasm and reunited with Gus, and I'd gotten through the waterfall, and I hadn't left the spider strand. Pride swelled in my chest, because I? I was fucking *awesome*, goddamn it.

I grinned at my self-congratulation, breathed another deep, deep breath, and sat up to straddle the strand. I'd just swung my left leg over to join the right one when a faint clatter beneath the water's roar made me pause. I knew that sound, I thought. That was—

It came again, and I stood up from the strand, my legs wobbly but holding as hope flared in me. I *should* know that sound, because I'd heard it often enough as my staff had struck the stone walls of the house during practice.

I turned toward the mouth of the cave and walked back toward the waterfall. Silhouetted against the faint light filtering through was Gus, sitting on a boulder. And at the base of that boulder, half in shadow, was the staff he must have knocked over. My staff. My last connection to Lucan and my reminder of why I was here and what I still faced.

The last, tattered vestiges of triumph drifted to the stone beneath my feet. Hot tears prickled behind my eyes. For a moment, I thought about giving in to them. I wanted nothing more than to curl up in a ball and give in to the exhaustion, the fear, the hurt …

The sheer misery.

But whatever it was that had kept me moving this far wasn't ready to give up just yet. Despite the staggering losses of friends and family and world, despite the seemingly insurmountable challenges of this damnable world I found myself in and the ones I would face if I ever made it to Camlann, despite everything, that dogged persistence in me lived on. It raised its head and nudged me, and damn the goddess to hell and back a thousand times …

It wouldn't let me give up.

And so I wet a corner of my already-damp cloak in the waterfall, scrubbed my face clean of the very thought of tears, collected my staff, and took stock of our surroundings. The spider strand that had brought us here continued into the belly of the cavern, toward a sliver of bright light. I hoped but knew better than to believe that might be the door to Camlann and, at this point, decided I'd settle for whatever we found there, as long as it meant we could be warm and dry.

"Ready?" I asked Gus.

He yawned in answer, and we set out together once more.

CHAPTER 17

I HADN'T COUNTED ON OPTICS. AS THE LIGHT AT THE END OF the tunnel got brighter, what lay around us became paradoxically darker, making the journey an exercise in patience. Gus did just fine with his feline vision, but with neither flashlight nor magick to light my way, I had to rely on good old-fashioned sense of touch, which mostly involved finding low spots in the ceiling with my head and obstacles along the path with my toes.

And swearing. A lot of swearing.

At about the halfway point, I stopped to adjust the rucksack strap across my collarbone where the wet canvas had chafed my skin. Was it just me, or was the air getting colder? Maybe it was just because my cloak was still damp, but—no. No, I was pretty sure that was snow I could smell. I sniffed experimentally. My nostrils promptly froze shut and my shoulders slumped. So much for warmer and drier at the other end.

Hesitating, I wrapped the folds of my cloak around me, trying to cover my fingers. The bottom corner that I'd wet for face-washing *thunked* against my ankle, frozen solid. Awesome. Just freaking awesome. Now what? Keep going? Go back? Sit here and cry after all?

Frankly, the last option held the most appeal, but the tears would freeze and make me even colder, and Gus had continued on ahead of me, so …

I shrugged. "Forward, ho!" I muttered under my breath. Then I rolled my eyes as I felt my way forward at a shuffle again. I really needed to work harder on my imaginary Edie so that I had someone besides myself to talk to.

I was still a good thirty feet from the end of the tunnel when I had to take a hand from under my cloak to shield my eyes from the light. My breath formed ice crystals in the air and froze to my cheeks, it was so cold here. Even though I had no plan B, I began to rethink the wisdom of continuing, and I called out to Gus, hoping to summon him back to me. But the cat neither answered nor returned, so I shaded my eyes, squinted against the light, and crossed the short distance remaining.

When I reached it, the opening wasn't much wider than the spider strand running through it. It was more of a crack in the mountainside than anything. To navigate it, I had to remove the rucksack, climb up on the strand, turn sideways, and suck everything in harder than I'd done since trying on my pre-pregnancy jeans after giving birth to Paul. I'd got the jeans done up at the time, but I'd pulled a muscle in my back and nearly passed out from lack of oxygen in the process. This went about the same.

I got wedged in so tightly at one point that real panic trickled through my veins. It took every argument I had to talk myself into exhaling the last of my precious air so that my lungs deflated by the needed quarter-inch, and when that still wasn't enough, to simply push through. I emerged on the other side in a writhing, wriggling kind of shimmy, inhaled a gulp of air, and once again pinwheeled wildly to keep from falling down another mountainside. This time, however, it wasn't into darkness but into the brilliant white light reflecting off a world of snow.

I STARED AT THE TABLEAU BEFORE ME AS MY HEART SANK TO ... no, it didn't sink. It shriveled. It shriveled up and sat in the hollow it left behind in my chest like a small, frozen raisin, and—

And my stomach growled at the analogy, because fuck,

what I wouldn't give for a raisin right now. Then my brain smacked my stomach upside its metaphorical head, because food was the last thing we should be concerned about—and it very well might be, given what lay before us, and …

I sagged against the stone wall I'd just emerged from and gazed across the snowbound landscape twenty feet below me. I stared at the single tree that sat at the center of the plateau, as white and icy as the land surrounding it. At the strand of black spider silk that bisected the plateau, passing the tree and continuing beyond. At the stark, towering, snow-dusted mountains that rose on every side, made of stone and crags and impossibilities and—

And fucking hell, I thought in a kind of numb disbelief. Really? Just how much harder was this trip through the Otherworld going to get, anyway?

A rumble ran through the ground beneath my feet, and I shrank back against the boulder and held the rucksack over my head as a hail of pebbles and fist-sized rocks slid down the mountain to land around me. They rolled and bounced into stillness, and after a moment, I lowered the rucksack and sent a baleful glance at the slopes above.

"Ask a stupid question …" I imagined Edie saying to me. She wouldn't have been wrong. I missed her. I missed the imaginary her, too. I missed … Gus. Oh hell. I was missing Gus.

I glanced around my immediate vicinity, but there was no sign of the cat either above or around me. Shading my eyes again, I peered down at the snowbound plateau below. Stared. Sighed. And swore at the trail of tiny footprints leading across the snow, parallel to the spider silk that passed beside the tree. I squinted harder. There. A small orange speck, trekking across the snow as if he hadn't a care in the world—and certainly no sense of his companion's vulnerability. I sighed.

We were going to have a discussion soon, my cat and I, about how some of us *didn't* have nine lives to squander. In the meantime, however …

Once more, I hiked up my cloak clear of my ankles and, using the staff as a walking stick, picked my way between rocks and down to the snowy plateau. I couldn't see Gus anymore when I arrived, but his tracks were clear, as was the silk strand beside them, so I took a firmer grip on the staff and stepped onto the snow—and promptly sank up to my knees in the stuff.

Ice crystals filled my boot. I expelled a hiss of air at the shock, wobbled for a second, and then pulled my foot back to firm ground. I leaned my butt against a nearby rock and unlaced the boot to empty it, but the sock within was already wet and the damage done. Resting the boot in my lap, I rubbed absently at one of the bumps on my head that I'd acquired in the tunnel and stared across the whiteness, my gaze tracing Gus's trail.

I wondered for a moment if he would return if I stayed here and waited, but no. No, he probably wouldn't. He would either continue on or wait for me wherever he was now, and then he would slowly freeze to death—alone—and so would I. And if we were both going to die, we might as well do so together, right?

With that morbid thought in mind, I put my boot back on and laced it, then stood, lifting with me my staff, the rucksack, and the weight of a resignation that grew heavier by the minute, despite my best efforts.

I wasn't looking forward to this next part.

CHAPTER 18

THE JOURNEY ACROSS THE PLATEAU WAS EVEN MORE MISERABLE than I'd anticipated. I tried not to dwell on it as I half plowed my way through the snow, but it became increasingly hard to ignore as more and more parts of me went from the painful pre-frozen stage to the numb, oh-hell-that's-not-good stage.

My toes went first; the rest of my feet followed. Unable to feel them beneath me anymore, I began stumbling and falling, which meant my hands kept plunging into the snow, too, and were next to lose their feeling—and then my forearms and shins, and, of course, my lips and nose. Lifting my limbs became harder with each inch of ground gained, and I resorted to crawling, pushing my hands forward and dragging my legs after. It wasn't unlike my trip through the first door into the Otherworld, I decided fuzzily. Just colder.

So much colder.

Until it wasn't.

Until there was no feeling at all ...

... and still I kept moving.

So focused was I on gaining a few inches at a time, and then an inch, and then a fraction of an inch, that when I fell forward into an emptiness, it took long, sluggish moments for my brain to register that the snow was gone. That I lay on hardened ground and grass made brittle by cold. That Gus climbed over my body and wound around my head and shoved at my shoulder with his own head. That his meowing became increasingly urgent the longer I lay still.

I couldn't make myself move for my own sake, but I did it for him. I hauled one unfeeling hand toward me and wedged it under my shoulder, then did the same with the other, noting with small surprise that I still gripped the staff in that one. Or perhaps it wasn't a surprise, because my fingers were probably frozen onto it.

I pushed up onto my hands and knees and swayed there a moment, with the ginger cat weaving in and out around my arms, his meowing unabated. Ahead of me—I blinked away a haze. Ahead of me stood the tree, its trunk massive and rough and more than half covered in frost. There was no snow at its base because the branches that spread out from it were so thickly interwoven and so wide that even without leaves, the snow could not penetrate. As shelter from the cold went, it was piss-poor, as Edie would have said, but it was better than nothing, and at least I could rest there.

Standing was out of the question, but after some trial and error, I managed to crawl to the tree without face-planting, and once there, to settle myself at its base with my back against the trunk. With fingers that felt like chunks of wood, I wrapped the cloak around me and huddled into its frozen folds.

And then the shivering started.

It was convulsive, wracking, and so ferocious that my jaw locked and my muscles screamed in agony. *Hypothermia*, I thought. *Shivering like this is one of the stages of hypothermia.* I remembered Jeanne educating all the mothers in the neighborhood about it one particularly cold winter, but I couldn't remember what stage shivering was, or what came after. My brain felt sluggish. Was that another sign? Probably, but between crossing the chasm, navigating the tunnel, and crawling through the snow, I was too tired to make myself think about it.

Rest, my body whispered to me. *Just for a while.*

My eyes drifted shut. The shivering slowed.

A weight landed against my chest, hard enough to jolt me back to awareness. And was it—growling? I forced my eyes open and found Gus's face thrust into mine. His ears were flat against his skull and his nose wrinkled in a snarl that bared his teeth as he yowled at me—a most unhappy yowl.

Shit. He was right. I roused myself and straightened my back against the tree trunk. If I slept, I would never wake. And while my body would keep Gus alive for a while—

My thoughts shied away from the idea. Hadn't I worried about that once before, a lifetime ago? No matter. I still wasn't keen on that particular end for myself.

Gus complained again.

"I'm working on it," I mumbled, pulling my focus back to the matter of survival. But how? The ring of mountains looked no more hospitable than the plateau I would have to cross to reach them in any direction, and—

A small, slowly spreading warmth drew my attention. Gus had curled up on my chest, and his heat had penetrated the cloak and my sweater beneath it. It reminded me of another heat, one that I carried at my core. A heat that Keven had made me promise not to call on and that the Weaver had advised against using, but now—now, it was my only chance. It was *our* only chance.

I wrapped my arms around my cat, burrowed my frozen face into his fur, and delved into my core.

I WOKE TO FIRE, A FACE FULL OF SMOKE, AND A FEMALE VOICE cursing in a language I didn't recognize. At least, given the tone and inflection, it sounded like it was cursing.

Caution advised that, in this unknown Otherworld, I should stay silent until I knew who—or what—I was dealing with, but the face full of smoke dictated otherwise. So did a coughing spasm.

I rolled from back to front and pushed myself up, eyes watering and lungs burning, turning my head and ducking this way and that in search of clean air. Just as I began to think none existed, the wind shifted, riffling through the hair at the back of my head and carrying the smoke with it. I sucked in welcome oxygen and my coughing subsided as I blinked away the sting of tears to find a woman crouched on the other side of a campfire about six feet away.

In spite of her pose, I could see that she was tall and slender, but in an athletic rather than a skinny way. Perhaps I was surmising the athletic part from the armor she wore. Firelight danced off polished metal elaborately wrought with symbols that veritably pulsed with a power I could sense even from here. The armor covered her arms and upper torso, and skintight brown leather encased her legs. Her skin was fair, weathered by sun and age and life, and she wore her long hair—faded strawberry blond streaked with gray—entwined in a braid that hung over one shoulder. And was that a sword lying on the ground beside her?

I froze as bright blue eyes lifted from the fire to meet my gaze, cold and hard and accusatory. She stared at me for a moment, then spat out something I didn't understand.

"I'm sorry—" I broke off to cough again, my throat dry and sore, then tried again. "I don't speak ..."

Whatever it is that you're speaking.

She rose to her feet—I'd been right about her being tall—and scowled down at me, her expression made fiercer by her face being partly cast now in shadow. "Just what, in the name of Asgard itself, were you trying to do? *Kill* it? Has it not suffered enough? If that cat hadn't come to my camp to get me, I'd be *hunting* your ass instead of trying to save it. I hope you appreciate that."

I blinked, my mind divided between the *Asgard* reference, the accusation, and the idea of Gus going for help.

"Uh ..." I said.

"You never did have any regard for anyone but yourself," she spat. "Selfish, *selfish* woman. Have you any idea of the damage you've already done? What you've allowed into our world while you were off gallivanting after that useless dick that calls himself a god? If Yggdrasil were to die—"

"Wait." I held up both hands to ward off her vitriol. "I'm not sure who you think I am, but I have no idea what you're talking about, and I certainly wasn't trying to kill anyone, let alone this Eeg—Eegdra—" I tried to replicate the syllables that had rolled off the woman's tongue. The name she'd spoken had sounded familiar, but where had I heard it? I sighed inwardly. This traipsing through the god world and overcoming insurmountable obstacles was playing havoc with my already not-stellar memory.

Eeg-dra-sill. Eegdrasill. Eeg—

"*Yggdrasill!*" I whispered. Yggdrasill, the Tree of Life. My gaze shot past the woman to the shadow of the tree looming behind her, just beyond the firelight. My breath caught as I took in the scorched earth that surrounded it, extending outward in a wide circle as far as I could see in the dark beyond. The skin along my arms prickled as I looked over one shoulder to confirm what I already knew—that the circle reached beyond me. That it centered on the tree under which I'd sheltered, centered on where I had been. I knew what had happened because I remembered what I'd done.

Fire. I'd called on my Fire to try and—

"You are exactly who I think you are. The *Morrigan*," the woman snapped. "You may have changed your appearance, but I would recognize the stench of crows about you anywhere."

Crows stank? I filed the question away with the backlog of others that grew with every moment I spent in the god world. I shook my head. "You're wrong. I'm not her," I said. "I'm not the Morrigan. At least, not entirely."

The woman's nostrils flared, and her head took on a threatening tilt. "You either are or you are not. You cannot be both."

"*Do or do not,*" said the voice of Yoda in my head, and I held back a snort that would probably have seen me decapitated. Pinching the bridge of my nose between finger and thumb, I debated how much to reveal to someone so obviously hostile to the goddess whose powers I held. Freaking hell, but the Morrigan had a lot to answer for, sending me in here with so little preparation. When I got back—*if* I got back—

"Well?" the woman demanded.

I sighed, dropping my hand back into my lap. "Claire," I said. "My name is Claire Emerson, and I'm human, and—"

"Impossible. No human can cross into our world."

"And I hold half the powers of the Morrigan," I finished. "And now I'd like to see my cat, please."

CHAPTER·19

"YOUR STORY IS ..." FREYA—FOR THAT WAS WHO SHE'D introduced herself as, although I'd already surmised as much —trailed off, seemingly at a loss for words as she regarded me across the dancing flames.

"Incredible?" I suggested, because even after all this time, it still felt that way to me when I stopped to think about it. As did finding myself rescued and being fed by Freya, wife of Odin and Norse goddess of love, fertility, battle, and death.

"That's one way to describe it, although I prefer impossible." Freya sliced off a bit of meat from the spit over the fire, speared it with the point of her knife, and leaned across to offer it to me, scowling as she did. I took it and popped it into my mouth, my eyes closing for a moment in sheer bliss, because meat. Real meat. And, oh my goddess, it was good.

The Weaver had told me that the only food in the Otherworld was ambrosia, but Freya had waved away the idea with a bark of laughter.

"As if any of us would have survived as long as we have with only that to eat and nothing to hunt. We would have gone madder than we already are," she'd said when I'd mentioned it. I had questions about that, too, of course, but given the darkness of her tone, I'd added them to the list.

I'd also insisted we locate Gus—I'd found him after a short search, loaf-shaped on a branch of Yggdrasil that overhung the fire—before I sat down at the fire and accepted food.

Freya herself had cooled a slice of the roasted carcass and set it on the branch of Yggdrasill occupied by the cat before settling herself on a blanket she spread across from me, one arm supporting her, the other resting on an upraised knee. She'd listened without comment while I told her about the war between the Crones and Morok, about the transfer of the pendant's power—half of the Morrigan's power—into me, about the splintering of the Earth world and the portal to Camlann that had been opened in my final battle with Morok.

The more I talked, the more I remembered—and found myself wanting—to tell her, in part because it felt good to unload on someone. And in greater part because, whatever her problem with the Morrigan might have been, her hostility toward me visibly diminished with every word, replaced by a speculation that sparked a tiny hope in me. If I could convince her that I was not the Morrigan herself, I thought, perhaps I might be able to ask her help in my quest. Goddess knew I could use an ally in this godforsaken world—no pun intended.

So when I finished the tale of my powers, I backtracked and filled in the gaps, telling her about the shades and the gnomes, the fire pixies and the goliath, the ether I knew as the Between, and—

"*No,*" the memory of Edie's voice whispered in my head, and I let my voice trail away into silence. She was right—or would have been if she were actually still with me. Lucan himself had once told me that the gods and goddesses were fickle at best, and as pleased as I was to see Freya softening toward me—and I still hoped I might gain her alliance—I could not fully trust someone I didn't know. Especially, if Lucan was right was also right, a goddess.

No, the bit about Morgana's magick, hidden in Camlann, would remain my secret.

Freya pried off what looked like a drumstick from the carcass and handed it across to me before taking the other for herself. For a while, we ate in a silence that was broken only by the snap and crackle of the fire. When she was done, she tossed the bone into the flames. I did likewise, then wiped my greasy fingers on the grimy denim covering my thighs. Not for the first time, I wished I had thought to bring a change of clothing with me.

Or at least clean underwear.

"Human," the Norse goddess mused, watching me through the flames between us. "But not."

I hadn't thought of myself in quite that way before. I would have preferred not to now. I shrugged. "Human," I corrected, "with half of the Morrigan's powers."

Across the fire, Freya stretched out on her side, propping herself up on one elbow. "Your words explain much about my world," she said. "The ether—what you call the Between— has made itself known here, too. Things come through—dark things like the ones you describe—whenever one of us disappears. They tear apart the world that is left behind."

The Weaver's words, all but forgotten in the days since I'd last seen her, came back to me. *"When one of those that your kind has placed here ceases to be, they leave their lands unprotected. When you release the ether with your destruction, it removes all but the skeleton of what was their place in this world."*

I repeated them to Freya, who grunted, presumably in agreement.

"What did she mean?" I asked. "About the ones my kind has placed here?"

Freya rolled onto her back and covered her eyes with one forearm. The shape that was Gus dropped out of the tree onto the frozen ground with a muffled thud and strolled over to curl up on the goddess's chest. Freya rubbed his ears for a moment, then tucked both arms beneath her head and stared up at the sky.

"We were once human, too," she said. "Did you know that?"

I regarded her through the flickering flames. "By *we*, you mean ..."

"The gods," she said. "All of us. As human as you or anyone else on your Earth—except that we knew magick. We could manipulate the elements, the energies, and that made us more in the eyes of others. It made us powerful. Mystical. And the more people believed in us, the more they feared and revered us, the greater our powers became—and the greater humankind's demands on us. Slowly, one at a time and out of desperation, I think, we found our way across the barrier into this, the Otherworld, and we each built our own lands within it."

Silence fell while her words settled into me and permeated the understanding I'd once held of the world I inhabited. I was remarkably unsurprised by them, I realized. Perhaps because of everything I'd already learned about the world of magick and gods. Perhaps because it just made sense. Especially the part about the demands made by humankind, which tracked as remarkably accurate.

"I see," I said. "And what about the disappearing part?"

"Belief," said the goddess. "Humankind's belief in us keeps us alive. When it fails, so do we. Our powers wane and we cannot maintain the world that we build for ourselves. We become weaker and more ... human, I suppose, and then we are gone."

She turned her head toward me. "At one time, the Otherworld was filled with us. We came from every corner of your world, and this place overflowed with life and power and magick. Now, you can travel days without seeing anyone. Eventually, once one of us has been gone long enough, the very fabric of the world we built falters—and then the dark creatures come."

Then, as I was mentally staggering under this new information, she frowned and murmured, "It's odd, really."

I swallowed a snort. Something in all of that was odder than the rest? The possibility seemed a bit far-fetched, but I'd bite. "What is?"

"I thought Odin and I were destined for the same," Freya continued, "We were declining the way others had done, but we seem to have enjoyed renewed strength these past few Earth years. I'm not sure why."

I thought about the Thor figurine tucked into the bottom of my rucksack, my grandson's good-luck charm pressed into my hand at our final goodbye. Braden's unflagging belief that it would keep me safe. His belief, period. But how in the world —in all the worlds for that matter—did one go about explaining the Marvel Universe to a goddess?

I decided it was easier not to attempt it and instead stared out into the dark shrouding the plateau. I thought about how far I had already traveled, and about the towering ring of mountains I would have to traverse if I continued on my quest to find Camlann.

"All the gods came here?" I asked.

"All."

"Even ..."

She chuckled. "Even that one."

"Huh," I said. "Just how big is this place, anyway?"

"It changes," replied the goddess. "It is what the Weaver makes it."

CHAPTER 20

"TELL ME ABOUT THE MORRIGAN," I SAID THE NEXT morning, watching as Freya fed the embers from the night before with the last of the branches that Yggdrasill had shed in an effort to save itself from my magick.

I reached cold, stiff hands out to the tiny flames, wishing I could just crawl into them. My cloak had provided next to no protection against either frozen ground or equally frozen air, and Freya, bless her goddess-y heart, had offered me neither her blanket nor her fur. I tried to put aside my grumpiness in favor of gleaning more information.

"Why do you dislike her so much?" I prodded.

Another long silence ensued. Freya, I was learning, was the master of long silences. I'd about given up on an answer and was contemplating—or more accurately, dreading—an attempt at coaxing my cranky hips to move when she spoke.

"You're lucky you're not her."

Yes, I'd already surmised that.

She glowered at me through the smoke rising from the fire that was struggling back to life. "Have you ever watched a man who claims to love you make an utter fool of himself over another woman?"

The question surprised a snort from me before I could catch it back. The goddess's blue eyes narrowed in annoyance, and I hastened to explain.

"Sorry," I said, "but actually … yes. I have."

She appraised me as if reevaluating my worth. Then she grunted. "And? What came of it?"

"He left me and married her. They have a baby, now."

"An infant? And he is your age?" She gave another grunt. "Then he has had his due."

I hadn't thought about it that way before, and the idea of Jeff losing sleep and dealing with the sheer energy of a baby made me laugh. "I suppose he has."

"My husband has not."

Oh, I thought. And then I put two and two together. "Oh," I said. "Odin and the Morrigan?"

"Not at first. At first, it was the Morrigan and Morok, until Morok dallied with another, and the Morrigan retaliated by bedding my husband." Freya sent me a look that was half sour and half murderous, and I stopped breathing for a moment until she seemed to remember that I wasn't actually her nemesis. She went back to poking the fire. "Morok returned to the Morrigan after the novelty wore off, of course, but she spurned him, preferring to keep her talons in Odin."

The goddess shot me another dark look, but my breath only hitched a bit this time, and I waited for her to continue.

"Morok, being the spoiled brat that he is—"

I gave another small snort, finding no lie in the sentiment. A spark of shared amusement flickered across Freya's expression.

"Exactly," she said. "Anyway, he crossed over to Earth in a huff and has proceeded to take out his displeasure on humankind ever since."

Again, I waited for her to go on, but she had begun packing the remains of last night's meal, wrapping it in a piece of questionable leather and putting it into an equally questionable leather pouch. I frowned, my own amusement evaporating like the smoke between us. That was it? That was the reason I was here? I'd learned many things in the god world that had taken considerable processing on my part to understand or, if I couldn't understand, at least to come to terms with. But this? The idea that the imminent destruction of my home, my family, my very planet was for no reason other than …

"Let me get this straight." Wanting my scowl to have more

impact—or at least be seen—I stood up to bring myself back to eye level with the goddess. Freya, finished with her story, was stamping out the remains of our fire, apparently done with me, too. "Are you telling me that this"—I waved my arms in a wide, all-encompassing circle over my head—"all of this is because of a *lover's spat?*"

Freya stared at me for a second, and then she threw back her head and guffawed. I mean, really *bellowed* with laughter. It took her forever to recover, too—or so it seemed to arms-crossed, toe-tapping me, who failed to see what was so freaking funny about any of it. The goddess gasped her way to a halt at last, wiping tears from her eyes with the back of one hand.

"I had never thought of it that way," she admitted, "but yes. Yes, I suppose it is."

"No," I said. "No. I refuse to believe that all of you are that petty."

"Then you are naive," she told me. "Did you not hear what I told you? About how we began? We were as human as any of you, Claire Emerson. *You're* the ones who insisted on placing us on pedestals. We've always fought amongst ourselves—for reasons of love, lust, revenge, greed, power. Whatever emotions you have, we have them, too. We can just create more of a mess with them because of who and what we are."

"And what about us?" I asked the goddess who had slung the blanket she'd used the night before over her horse. "Didn't you care at all about what Morok was doing?"

"Of course we did." Freya topped the blanket with the fur, then picked up a small leather saddle from beside the remains of the fire and set it over both. "We held a council meeting. The Morrigan was deemed responsible for stopping Morok and sent after him."

Council … deemed responsible … I gaped at the goddess. "That—that's it? That was your solution?"

"Not mine. The council's." She cinched the saddle into place. "If it had been up to me, I would have hauled his ass back here and imprisoned him. It wasn't up to me."

"But what about since then? What about now? Can't this council—"

"There is no more council, Claire Emerson. Half of them are gone—vanished—and the other half are waiting for their own time to come. We, all of us here, are a dying breed, just as humans are. The difference is that you care. We don't."

IN THE END, FREYA TOOK PITY ON ME AND TRANSPORTED ME AS far as the base of the mountains, her horse plowing easily through the snowy plateau in a fraction of the time it would have taken me to walk the same distance. She remained astride as I slid from the horse's back, then handed me my staff and rucksack. Gus unwrapped himself from her shoulders and jumped down onto the horse's haunches, then to the ground. The big animal didn't so much as flinch.

Freya cleared her throat as I slung the rucksack over my shoulder and arranged the strap over the folds of my tattered cloak. I looked up.

"The strand you follow …" she said.

"Yes?"

"It will pass through my husband's lands."

"Odin?"

"Odin," she agreed.

I felt my eyebrows twitch together, probably because my skin was stiff with cold again. The air here was no warmer than it had been on the plateau, and I already dreaded the climb ahead. "And that's a problem because …?" I asked.

"Like me, he will sense the Morrigan in you. You might

not be given a chance to explain. And even if he does listen …
"

"He won't care," I finished.

"Oh, he will care very much. He has never forgiven her for spurning him."

Awesome. Just fucking awesome.

"What do I do?"

"Find another way."

"What do I do if that's not an option?" I clarified, ever mindful of the Weaver's instructions.

The Norse goddess stared up the mountain as her mount shifted beneath her and snorted vapor into the air. Then she sighed and reached into the pouch she wore at her waist.

"If you can convince him to hear your story, he will invite you to tell it over dinner. Then, if he believes you, he will ask a favor of you in return for granting you passage. You must refuse, no matter how angry he seems. He will get up from the table and pace the room, and when he isn't looking, put this into his drink. If you're lucky, it will buy you enough time to slip away and pass out of his lands."

She held out a small, glass vial that glowed a faint amber. "It must go into his wine, nothing else. If you put it in anything other, its taste will give it away."

"That's an awful lot of *ifs*," I said, eyeing the vial. "Could you not just come with me and make him listen? Help me get past him?"

"I could," she said, gathering up the reins. "But I will not. This is your war, not mine."

"Wait," I said. "What about on the other side? Will I find Camlann on the other side of his land, or is there someone else—another god?"

"I have never been beyond the wall." Freya shrugged armored shoulders. "I do not know what lies there."

My pulse kicked up a notch as excitement sparked in me. "Wall? There's a wall?"

"There is. Or there was, the last time I was there. Perhaps the Weaver has changed that, too. Again, I do not know."

It was still the best news I'd had since entering the god world. I'd take it. And I'd hold onto it for dear life. I nodded acknowledgement and said, "Thank you. For saving me and—"

"I saved Yggdrasill," she cut in. "You were just there."

Oh.

"Well, thank you anyway," I said. "For not letting me die. And for bringing me here."

The corner of her mouth twitched upward, and she inclined her head. "You are welcome."

She urged the horse forward, then wheeled it around to face me again. "One last thing. These mountains were the land of Zeus and Hera and their kin at one time, but they have long been gone. There will likely be dark things here"— she nodded up the slope—"that have come from the ether. You will do well to be vigilant."

Dark things from the ether. My mind instantly conjured images of the shades, and I shuddered. Was that why Freya wouldn't take me any further? If the shades were here …

"Have you seen them?" I asked. "What do they look like?"

"I have not."

"But I thought you said your lands and Odin's were this way."

Freya gave a short bark of laughter. "I have seen neither my husband nor his lands since he chose to betray me with the Morrigan, nor will I," she said. " I do, however, hope you win your war, Claire Emerson. Farewell."

114

CHAPTER 21

VIGILANT DIDN'T BEGIN TO DESCRIBE MY LEVEL OF PARANOIA AS
Gus and I laboriously climbed the mountain. Well, my climb
was laborious. Gus, on the other hand, trotted ahead with his
usual stamina, fueled, no doubt, by all the meat Freya had
given him the night before.

As on the mountain I'd fallen down when we arrived in
the Otherworld, nothing moved here. There were no plants,
no animals, no insects. That didn't stop me from jumping at
every shadow and imagined sound beneath the ceaseless wind
that blew across the slopes. I remembered all too well the
razor-sharp feathers and yellow eyes of the hell-beasts called
shades, and I didn't care for my chances of survival if we
encountered one here. Not even with—or perhaps especially
with—my magick.

Whatever danger might be lying in wait for us, however,
we'd only been climbing for half an hour or so when I realized
it wasn't going to be shades.

We'd reached a rockier-than-the rest-of the-mountain
place that culminated in a small plateau. As I stepped down
from between two boulders, my foot connected with something that rolled a few feet away before coming to rest against
the desiccated remains of a shrub. The object's lack of weight
or substance caught my attention. I followed it, careful not to
let the spider strand out of sight, and stooped to peer down at
the round, pale, whitish gleam. Was that ... what I thought
it was?

Using the tip of my staff, I poked at it until it turned it
over, and then I stumbled back, almost tripping over Gus,
who'd come to sniff at what I'd found. My gaze locked on the
skull staring up at me with huge eye sockets on either side of

what was unmistakably a broken beak. *A bird*, I tried to tell myself. *It's only a bird.*

But I had seen no birds. Not anywhere. Not once since I'd crossed the threshold into the Otherworld, even in the forest where the Weaver had her home. And if there were no birds …

My gaze shifted left and settled on a long, black feather poking out from the rocks nearby. Then on others scattered near it. I didn't have to go closer to know that they would be razor-edged. Or to know where they'd come from. Shades. Fucking hell.

Another skull lay near the feathers, and when I looked closer, there was another beyond that, and another beyond that, and suddenly, they were everywhere, some drifted with snow, others swept bare of it by the wind. I panned the barren plateau with mounting horror, wondering how I could have missed seeing them. Stepping on them. There were dozens. An entire—did shades travel in flocks?

I shivered and drew my cloak closed against the wind that tried to crawl under my sweater. Freya had been right to warn me that the creatures from the ether might have broken through to Zeus's lands, but she'd obviously hadn't known that something else was here. Something that was capable of slaughtering a small army of shades.

The question was, had it caught them all?

And the other question was, where was *it* now?

I didn't care to remain to find out. With a last look around the plateau, I retraced my steps to the Weaver's strand, careful to avoid the skulls this time, and began my climb again, my steps somewhat more cautious than they'd been before. Abject fear will do that to a person.

A few paces ahead of me, Gus stopped in his tracks, his back arched and his tail three times its normal size. A low growl rumbled in his throat. I'd barely registered his warning when he bolted to the left, through a crevice in the rocks, and disappeared.

"Gu—" I slapped a hand over my mouth in mid shout. Whatever had spooked the cat, it might be smart not to draw its attention. I took my hand away and hissed, *"Gus!"* but the wind whipped my words back into my face and the crevice— as far as I could see into it—remained empty of cat.

I shifted my weight from one foot to the other and back again, wrestling with my instinct to follow. The hand not holding my staff traced the spider strand we'd been following, then closed over it in a fierce grip. The Weaver's words came back to me.

"You must not leave it. If you do, you will be lost forever."

"Damn you, Merlin-Mergan-Gus," I muttered. "Get your fuzzy butt back here. *Now.*"

But neither his fuzzy butt nor the rest of him returned. Long seconds dragged into longer minutes, and I grew cold from standing in the bitter wind. Colder from the brutal decision facing me. I couldn't risk going after the cat. I knew that. Too much depended on me finishing this task the Morrigan had given me. Too *many* depended on it.

But neither could I stay here and wait for him. I wouldn't survive the cold, and that would bring me back to not finishing my task. Not getting to Camlann. Not finding Lucan or Morok.

Another few minutes slipped past while I stared at the crevice and willed Gus to come back. And then, then I could wait no more. I swiped tears from my cheeks. I would have to go and trust that he'd find me again … if he could.

Feeling as if I'd left a chunk of my heart bleeding on the ground behind me, I turned toward the spider strand and began my lonely climb up the desolate mountain, counting my steps to distract myself, a trick I'd once used to keep Paul occupied on long hikes.

Ten, eleven, twelve …

Damned cat.

I sniffled and wiped my cheeks again.

Twenty-three, twenty-four …

Damned beautiful, precious, amazing—

An unholy scream tore through my solitude. My head whipped around, and I stared back down the mountain at the crevice, barely visible from here. The scream came again, and my heart gave a huge, adrenaline-fueled thud. *Gus.*

I was in the crevice before I had time to think. Through it before I had time to think better of it. And emerging on the other side before I saw—and almost fell into—the enormous creature with huge wings that beat at the air, hovering just above the ground in front of me.

Its head was the size of a Saint Bernard—as in the entire dog—and its body was disproportionately dump-truck sized and covered in thick, scaly, gray-blue skin. A double row of jagged teeth filled its mouth, some missing, others broken, and beady red eyes were focused on the rocks to my left. I had just enough time to decide that it looked like a cross between a reptile and a bird—like a dinosaur—before the beady gaze swiveled to fix on me. A blast of hot, fetid air slammed into me, fire followed in its wake, and I threw myself sideways into the shelter of a rock.

Holy hell, I thought in shock. Not a dinosaur. A dragon. An honest-to-god, fire-breathing, freaking dragon. I cowered behind my makeshift shield as fire streamed around and over me. The rock broke the flames, but just barely—and it was becoming uncomfortably hot at my back. If I stayed here, I would be roasted alive. The blast dissipated, and I popped my head up to take stock of my surroundings. I had only a second, so my scan was fast. Focused. And not promising.

First, dear goddess, that thing was huge! Second, if I retreated into the crevice, there was nothing to stop it from following me. Third, I had nowhere else to hide. And fourth … Gus.

The orange cat crouched on a rock outcropping at eye level with the dragon, his face scrunched up in a feline hiss and the ridge of hair along his back standing on end. The difference in size between him and his aggressor was ridiculous, but despite the fact that the impossible standoff could only end one way, the cat was holding his ground. I had no time to decide whether he was brave or stupid, though, because the dragon's beady gaze zeroed in on him again, and without thinking, I yelled, "Hey!"

Red eyes swiveled back to me even as I registered my mistake.

My likely fatal mistake.

Fuck.

In slow motion, I watched the dragon's head rear back. Its mouth opened wide, and its chest swelled with air and deadly intent. Faced with becoming a human torch as an alternative, I threw caution to the wind that snatched relentlessly at my cloak and hair.

Because not just fuck but *fuck it.*

I'd done my best to play by the rules in this world, damn it. I'd stayed the course, I'd followed the Weaver's strand as instructed and, with the single exception of unintentionally almost killing the Tree of Life itself, I'd heeded her and Keven's warnings about not using my magick.

My very human, very limited sixty-year-old body had taken every step solo. It had been beaten and battered and damned near drowned and then frozen, and now it was going to fry? I didn't think so, because ...

Fuck.

It.

The dragon spewed flames in my direction again. Forgetting about aching joints and words of warning and rules and everything except the power I carried in my core, I slammed aside the inferno with my staff, sending it back toward the creature. Its own fire engulfed its wings, and it somersaulted in the air, shrieking with pain. I didn't want to wait to see what might come next. I had no idea what equated to the Earth element here, but I'd been able to draw on Water when I was with the Weaver, and Fire before I'd met Freya, so surely I could find something similar here. Something that would—oh, I don't know—maybe let me drop a freaking mountain on this monster.

High overhead, the dragon gave a mighty beat of its wings and extinguished the flames.

I set the end of my staff against the ground and widened my stance, then drew my focus inward and sent it to the soles of my feet. At first, I felt nothing and alarm flickered through me as the dragon screamed again, but this time in rage. Had I been wrong? Should I shift to a different element? But which one? I looked up at the winged menace hurtling toward me, dagger-like rear claws extended and mouth agape.

I tightened my grip on the staff. Shifted my feet. Closed my eyes. Another scream came from above. I ignored it and stilled my mind, my panic, my core. And then I felt it. It was like the Earth element, but deeper than Earth had been, and bigger. So much bigger. I braced myself and sent my roots down, down ... there. Connection bucked through me. Power coursed in its wake. I pushed away the fear that belonged to Claire and fell into the exhilaration that sang through the Morrigan part of me. She knew this power. Knew what to do with it.

I straightened my free arm at my side, holding it palm open and facing the ground. The god world's Earth element surged up through my feet and through the staff and raced through my body to gather in that open palm. My muscles tensed. Spasmed. Went rigid. The Morrigan in me demanded that I raise the hand and direct the power at the dragon. The Claire body she shared could not.

It was too much, I thought dazedly. Maybe if I'd been more rested, younger ...

Less human, whispered the power.

I looked up. The dragon was a dozen feet away. So close that I could smell the stench of singed wings and once again feel the heat of its breath, and—no. There had to be another way. I still had to find Lucan, and I would not, could not give up.

I stopped trying to lift my arm and focused entirely on the ground at my feet. The god world's power flowed into me, coursed up through my staff and legs, flowed to my open hand, pooled, gathered, built ...

And then, as the dragon reached for me and my vision filled with claws and glistening scales, I sent the power back into the ground. All of it, all at once, in one massive surge. The mountain shuddered and rumbled beneath me, and the very air itself seemed to tremble. The dragon back-beat with its injured wings but couldn't slow its descent. Not enough. Not in time.

The mountain collapsed on it—and on me.

CHAPTER 22

"YES, YES. WE FIND," A WOMAN'S VOICE SAID CHEERFULLY AS I surfaced back into consciousness. It sounded close but muffled, and it had an accent that I couldn't place as—

Wait. I'd surfaced into consciousness but not into light. Why hadn't I surfaced into light? I blinked to be sure my eyes were open. They were, but they were also filled with grit that scratched with every flutter of my eyelids. And it was as dark as night. Or, more accurately, I thought as I remembered the mountain's collapse and became aware of a huge weight across my chest, as dark as being buried alive.

Panic clawed at my throat, and I wriggled my right arm free to claw at the rock lying on me. Then I recoiled in horror when I realized it wasn't a rock at all. It was something else. Something pliable beneath my fingers. Scaly.

Freaking hell, it was the dragon. I opened my mouth to yell for help but caught it back and poked again at the dragon. It didn't respond, and I realized that it was cold to the touch. I supposed it was possible that it might be cold-blooded to begin with, but the fact that it didn't move made me think that it was simply …

Dead.

I moaned. I had a dead dragon lying on me, and half a mountain's worth of rock covering both of us, and if the cheerful voice was alone, it didn't stand much of a chance of digging me out, and dear goddess, I'd been buried alive.

The cheerful voice, heavily accented, came again, "You here?" it asked. Or maybe it was, "*You hear?*"

Either way, my response was the same. "I'm here!" I called back, and then for good measure, I added, "And yes, I can hear you!"

"I here, too," it replied comfortably. "You wait. I dig."

There was little else I could do, pinned under a dragon and half a mountain, and so I closed my gritty, watery eyes, focused on my breathing (which wasn't easy with a dead dragon and half a mountain sitting on my chest), tried not to imagine all the fates that might have befallen my cat, and strained to hear evidence of my imminent rescue.

For the longest time—hours, it seemed, or maybe weeks— I heard nothing but the pulse of my own blood in my ears. It brought back unpleasant memories of the time Morok had left me to die in the cell from which Lucan and I had rescued Elysabeth. I tried to push the memories away, but that only opened the door to a flood of other Morok memories: a destroyed Earth house and lifeless Keven, the fever that nearly consumed Lucan, Natalie lying in a coma, the Crones held captive as Morok drained their powers from them, the deaths of hundreds of New Yorkers when he began opening a portal and let in the creatures from the Between, the last battle that I had both won and lost ... having to say goodbye to my family and friends forever.

Damn, but the dark god had a lot to answer for.

And, double damn, but lying trapped in the dark wasn't what I'd call good for my mental health. I took a shaky breath. I still couldn't hear any sounds from the outside world. Was my would-be rescuer still there? I flexed the fingers of my left hand, the one that had pushed the elemental power back into the god world's soil. Maybe I should—

Everything in me—thoughts, memories, ideas of escape, everything—ground to a standstill and focused on the fingers I'd just tried to move. Tried being the operative word. Because while they'd twitched, they'd also resisted my effort, and not because of anything weighing them down. More like ...

"No," I whispered. I tried to move the rest of me, and horror spawned in my chest and spread like tentacles through my lungs, my belly, my bowel. *No, no, no.*

But yes. My fingers were rooted in the very ground they'd cast their magick into. In the soil of the god world itself. And so were my feet.

EVEN AS MY PREDICAMENT SANK IN, HOWEVER, THE WEIGHT ON my chest lifted, sudden light filled my near-tomb, and strong hands seized my shoulders and tried to pull me upright.

"Wait!" I exclaimed. "My hand—my feet—"

But the pulling had already stopped, and as I blinked away the rest of the grit and my eyes adjusted to the new light, a woman's broad, creased face peered down at me.

"You stuck," she announced. "Is not good."

"No," I agreed faintly, because an all-new panic had set in. "It's not good."

I'd been "stuck" once before. It had been the first time I'd connected with the Earth element in the cellar of the house, when the unflappable Keven had taken on the task of teaching me magick and I'd promptly rooted my feet to the floor. That had been terrifying enough. But this? Being stuck at three points instead of just two, unable to even sit up, with no gargoyle to offer words of counsel or calm, and with a stranger's wrinkled visage peering down at me?

The visage grunted. "I have tools. I get."

Before I could draw breath to object or ask how long she would be or what tools she had in mind, the old woman disappeared, leaving me to stare up at the sky, the rocks piled around me, and the dead dragon's head dangling over the latter with its tongue hanging out, inches from my face. My skin crawling, I retreated as far away as I could wriggle and tugged, again with no success, at my hand and feet. A quiet dread unfurled in my belly.

Once, I'd worried that I would die in the Earth house

cellar. In retrospect, the possibility seemed downright comforting, because there, at least, someone would have eventually found me. But here? In the Otherworld? My death would go unnoticed. I would never be found. And no one would know that I hadn't even made it to Camlann.

Little tentacles spread outward from the dread, reaching for my lungs. I took a deep, steadying breath and choked on the scent of dead dragon—a rather indescribable odor somewhere between burnt eggs and the inside of a forgotten gym bag. I breathed again, through my mouth this time.

I was panicking over nothing, I told myself. I'd defeated Morok himself, for heaven's sake, and moved an entire house not once, but twice—complete with occupants—and I'd traveled the ley lines by myself, and I had half the powers of the Morrigan. Surely to goodness that meant I could figure out how to get myself unstuck.

Ignoring the dragon tongue lolling above my head, I turned my focus inward, seeking the connections I'd forged with the god world. I found the one in my hand first, then those in my feet, and followed them outward, downward, downward some more ... and more ... and—

I frowned. Something wasn't right. The connections went too deep. They felt foreign, as if ...

A chill swept through me. As if they weren't mine. As if whatever I'd tapped into with my powers, whatever I'd drawn on, had reversed the flow. *It* held *me* instead of the other way around. I had no control over it.

That was it. I was done. I really was going to die here.

My panic returned—and then my would-be rescuer did, too.

CHAPTER 23

MY RELIEF AT SEEING THE SQUAT FIGURE REAPPEAR WAS SHORT lived as I saw the weapon she swung from one hand. Was it just my imagination, or did that thing look like something the Grim Reaper might carry?

"Um … what is that for?" I pointed at it with my free hand.

"I cut loose." She indicated my legs with her other hand.

I stared at her, trying to make her words make sense. Helpfully, she demonstrated her intention by drawing a finger of her free hand across the wrist of the one holding what looked like a scythe. Less helpfully, she added a *snick* sound.

I recoiled with a yelp. "You cut—you want to *cut me*? With that? Oh, no. No. Absolutely not. No cut. No."

I threw myself against my invisible bonds, determined to free myself before the crazy woman tried. But the power binding me to the ground grew stronger with every effort, and I soon exhausted what little energy I had. I gave up and laid back again, panting as I stared at the woman waiting patiently above me. She really *was* insane.

She hefted the weapon onto her shoulder, and I got a better look at it. It was definitely a scythe.

"Is magick," she said. "Cut uzzer magick."

I hesitated. The scythe was magick? Why couldn't she have led with that? I eyed the weapon, which still looked far too real for my taste. I really wasn't keen on taking a stranger's word for this but, on the other hand, I couldn't very well stay bound to the ground beside a dead dragon for the rest of my life, either.

Seeming to take my silence for consent, the woman took a two-handed grip on the lethal-looking tool and swung it up like a baseball bat. I was pretty sure that wasn't how one used a scythe, but—

"You close eyes," she said.

I didn't need to be told twice. My eyes squeezed shut of their own accord as the scythe arced down toward my leg and I wondered how long it took to bleed to death.

Light flared as I felt the metal blade slice through my left ankle. It was brilliant enough to cause spots behind my eyelids when it faded, but not brilliant enough to distract me from my surprise at the utter lack of pain. Maybe that came later, when the nerves realized they'd been severed?

"Uzzer one now," the woman said cheerfully.

Another flare of light. More spots. A slightly hysterical part of me wondered what would have happened if I hadn't closed my eyes in time. A much more hysterical part wondered why the first part was being so calm about it all.

"Now hand," announced my rescuer.

Light flared again, the woman grunted, and then a strong hand seized mine and hauled me out of the rock pit. I promptly collapsed to the ground.

"You're *insane*," I whispered, my legs shaking so hard that I thought I might never stand up again. I huddled into the folds of my filthy cloak, searching for a warmth and comfort that it no longer held. Its magick had worn out at last, and it had nothing left.

I could sympathize.

The corpulent woman rested her scythe on the ground and leaned on its handle, tucking her other hand into the pocket of the apron tied around her waist.

"I not insane. I Baba Yaga," she told me proudly.

I gaped. I'd just been rescued by the witch of Russian folk-tale fame? "Baba Yaga? *The* Baba Yaga?"

She grinned an almost-toothless grin at me. "You know me. Is good."

My nerves would beg to differ after that scythe-thing, but I nodded. "I know you, yes. But you're not a god—how did you get here?"

Baba Yaga wrinkled her nose and snorted. "Many peoples believe in Baba Yaga. Beink witch is much better than beink god. You are witch, too?"

"It's ..." I sighed. I was back to that catchphrase again, wasn't I? Perhaps if I survived this, I'd just have it tattooed on my forehead. "It's complicated," I said.

"Is no matter." The old witch shrugged. "Is only important you live, and now you take dragon baby."

"Now I—excuse me?" I forgot about my shaky legs and clambered to my feet. Despite the ache in my hips and back making me stoop like an old woman, I towered over Baba Yaga by a good foot. The famed witch was short, nearly as wide as she was tall, and absolutely ancient in comparison to my version of old, but she seemed unfazed by either my relative youth or her lack of height.

"Dragon baby," she repeated, pointing a finger. "You take."

I followed her finger toward Gus, and my heart leapt with joy at the welcome sight of my orange companion. Then I noticed that his ears were laid flat against his skull, and that a wide-eyed ball of blue fluff was snuggled in beside him. An instinctive *awww* formed in my throat, but I squelched it mercilessly. Because no. I didn't care how fluffy (it was *so* fluffy) or cute (it was adorable) it might be. There would be no dragon, baby or otherwise, coming with me. The last thing I needed was another responsibility in my life right now.

"No." I put on my most ferocious scowl and shook my head at the witch. "Absolutely not. No baby dragon. No."

Baba Yaga shrugged. "Cat is muzzer now. You take."

Muzzer? As in a dragon by anuzzer muzzer? I stifled a *snerk* of laughter that would have ruined my scowl.

"Cat is good." Baba Yaga leaned down and patted Gus on the head hard enough to flatten him, but he was too preoccupied with hissing at the blue fluff to notice. "Dragon fozzer is dick and kill muzzer. Cat save baby. Baby like cat. Cat is new muzzer. You is cat's muzzer. You take baby."

She meant mother, all right. Somehow, she'd decided that Gus was the dragon's new mother because he'd saved him— her—it—from the homicidal dragon father. And I'd come after him and saved him, and—

"No," I said again. "You don't understand. I can't take it. Not where I'm going. I'm not even sure I'll *get* where I'm going. Or that I'll survive when I get there." I spread my hands in a gesture of helplessness. "I can't possibly be responsible for another—"

"You take," Baba Yaga said equably, as if I hadn't even spoken. She hefted the massive scythe in one hand and swung it up to rest on her shoulder, then started across the slope toward—was that a house?

On *chicken legs?*

The witch's voice carried back to me on the wind. "Come. I feed."

I stared after her as she hobbled up the crooked steps of the equally crooked house—which teetered precariously on its two legs before righting itself—and disappeared inside. Exhaustion, disbelief, and rebellion mingled together in an orneriness that I hadn't felt in years.

"You're not the boss of me," I wanted to yell after her, but now that the aftereffects of the scythe-triggered adrenaline rush were wearing off, my ribs hurt too much to take the necessary deep breath. Everything hurt too much, come to think of it, and that just made my frustration spike higher.

I looked around for something to kick, but all I could find were stones, which would only add to my injuries, and the dead dragon, which would be a level of *eww* that I wasn't comfortable with. My inclination toward violence faded as my gaze settled on Gus and the fluff ball nestled against him.

Gus, who had been my loyal, uncomplaining companion

through all the challenges we'd faced in this world of insanity. Gus, who hadn't eaten since the meal he and I had shared with Freya beneath the spreading branches of Yggdrasill. Gus, who had saved a baby dragon that I was absolutely not taking with me but also still needed to eat, poor thing.

My own stomach rumbled at the thought of food, and I gave up.

"Oh, for fuck's sake," I growled at cat and fluff. "You heard the woman. Food."

I snatched up the staff that Baba Yaga had leaned against the dead dragon's belly, stepped over the long, limp tail, and led the way toward the crooked house on chicken legs. As I stomped past the pile of rubble, I couldn't help but be in awe of how much Baba Yaga had removed to get at me—or to shudder at how much I'd thrown at the dragon to stop it. Far more than I'd intended, just as the Fire I'd called on had been more, too. And the Water at the Weaver's—

A splash of bright green at the corner of my eye stopped me in my tracks and knocked the breath from my lungs in a soft, strangled, "Oh."

A second dragon lay crumpled, its body the same color as the one I'd killed, in a pool of bright green that darkened around the edges as it dried. It was blood, I realized, putting a hand to my suddenly queasy stomach. Dragon blood. My gaze picked out tufts of blue poking out from beneath the dragon, along with shards of opalescent shells from the eggs that had been smashed. They and their contents also swam in the lake of green, and my heart contracted sharply. This was the mother that Baba Yaga had spoken of. A mother that had died trying to protect her young with her own body.

Unexpected grief tightened my throat, and I blinked back a prickle of tears. Then I looked over my shoulder to where a ball of fluff rolled in Gus's wake, chirruping anxiously as it tried to keep up with him. The sole survivor of the massacre. The cat would definitely get extra scritches for this—along with whatever tidbits he wanted from whatever dinner Baba Yaga gave me.

I turned back toward the house, straightened my battered spine, and scowled.

But I was still damned if I was taking a baby dragon with me.

CHAPTER 24

"BUT WHAT AM I SUPPOSED TO FEED IT? AND *HOW* AM I supposed to feed it? I don't even have food for myself or Gus." I sat at a small table in the single room of Baba Yaga's house, trying not to drool too much as the delicious scent of meat wafted from the small, pot-bellied stove where she worked.

Both table and room were cluttered with paraphernalia that appeared to have been collected over millennia: pots, pans, ceramic bowls and dishes—most chipped or cracked— sat on shelves and counters; herbs filled bottles and jars and hung in bunches from rafters thick with dusty cobwebs; clothing hung from hooks lining the wall; and odds and ends I couldn't identify filled nearly every other surface and gap.

It would take a month of Sundays to take stock of the witch's possessions, a lifetime to clean them. Right now, however, I was focused solely on her broad back as she ladled stew into a bowl from a cauldron on the stove—and on the argument I could feel myself losing, one implacable parry of my words at a time.

"Rrrats," Baba Yaga answered my question placidly, rolling her *r* as she leaned down and patted out the flames licking at her trouser bottoms. It was the third time the dragon baby had sneezed, and the third time it had set fire to something.

Yet another reason I didn't want to—*couldn't*, I corrected myself—take it with me.

I scowled at Baba Yaga as she placed the stew in front of me.

"Rats?" I echoed.

"*Da.* Cat will catch." She set another bowl on the floor for Gus, who snatched a chunk of meat from the broth and

hunched over it, growling when the fluff-ball that had adopted
him came too near. Baba Yaga fished a second piece of meat
from the bowl, squished it between her fingers, and set it in
front of the dragon, who sniffed at it suspiciously.

"Dragons eat rats?" I thought about the big male I'd killed
—and the smaller but still huge muzzer—and tried to imagine
how many rats had to inhabit the mountain to keep beasts of
that size alive. The place must be crawling with them, the
possibility of which made my skin crawl. I eyed the stew with
suspicion and tucked the folds of my cloak around my feet as I
peered into the room's cluttered corners.

"*Baby* dragon eat rrrats," said Baba Yaga, straightening up
and wiping her fingers on her work-stained apron. "Later, eat
goat. Bear. Shade."

"Dragons can kill shades?" So that's what was responsible
for the bone yard I'd walked through. I perked up at the idea.
If I ever made it to Camlann, a shade-devouring dragon
might come in handy. "How long before it's big enough for
that?"

"Year. Two. Mebbe s'ree." Baba Yaga shrugged. "For now,
rrrats."

So much for that brief idea. I went back to shaking my
head. "No. I really, really can't. I still have so far to go just to
get *to* Odin's lands, let along through them, and then I have to
find Lucan and Morok and the—" I bit down on the word
magick, remembering just in time that I wasn't sharing that
knowledge with anyone—not even Grandmother Witch here.

Baba Yaga wiped her hands on her apron front and placed
them on her ample hips. She regarded me for a moment with
a glimmer in her eye that I didn't like.

"Odin far," she said. "Very far."

"You've been there? To his land?"

"Baba Yaga house go everywhere."

"How far is it, exactly?"

"Too far for you." She waved a hand at my disheveled

state, and I swore I felt the ache in my bones intensify. "You not make it. House, on uzzer hand ..."

I wanted to argue. I really did. But when I thought about what I'd already come through, what had already nearly killed me, and the mountain range I had yet to traverse, I had to admit she was right. My sixty-year-old body was nearing done, and without the magick that I obviously couldn't trust in this world, I wasn't going to survive.

Plus, there was the little matter of finding my way back to the spider strand the Weaver had said that I would lose forever if I strayed from it. If she'd been right, I could wander around this mountainside forever. Or until I died of cold. Or a shade got me. Or, or, or.

I glanced down at the ball of fluff that was licking the floor clean where the witch had put the meat for him, and I felt the proverbial noose closing around me. Then I met the glimmer in Baba Yaga's eye and sighed.

"What do you propose?" I asked.

The witch rewarded my question with a broad, toothless smile, and just like that, I lost the argument.

As exhausted as I was, I didn't expect to sleep while we traveled, in good part because there was no actual bed (Baba Yaga, it turned out, had no need of sleep). I ended up curled into a ball on a pile of aprons on the floor with Gus tucked against my back and the ball of fluff snuggled into my chest. A tiny vibration rumbled through him.

"Is he *purring*?" I asked the old witch who sat at the table, playing a solitary game of cards.

"Cat is muzzer," she replied without looking up. "He sink he is cat now."

I mulled over the response, my fatigue-fogged brain

knowing it meant something but struggling to—aha. "Gus was the first thing he saw coming out of the egg," I said, inordinately proud of myself for figuring it out. "He imprinted on him."

"*Da*." She nodded.

The implications of that sank in, and I grimaced. Oh, the cat was just going to love that, especially as the dragon outgrew him. Poor Gus.

"How long will it take to get there?" I asked.

"You sleep, we z'ere."

That soon? I wondered for a moment if I'd been duped, but when I looked out the window above me, I saw the scenery racing past. I knew that each enormous stride of the house's chicken legs ate up more ground than I could have covered in half a day of walking. And speaking of covered ...

I eyed the cloak I'd left hanging over the back of Baba Yaga's chair. It was stiff with caked dirt and green blood and smelled of my sweat and being entombed with a dead dragon. I hadn't particularly wanted to have it covering me while I slept, in case it provoked nightmares. But now, between the cold of the floor beneath me and the cold that came with my fatigue, I was chilled to the bone.

"Can I trouble you to pass me my cloak?" I asked the witch, not wanting to disturb either Gus or fluff.

Baba Yaga stood and lifted the cloak from the chair. Her already-lined face wrinkled up even more. "Is dirty," she announced. "Stinky."

"I know, but—"

She shook out the cloak's folds, held it by one edge, and gave the garment a brisk snap in the air. She sniffed it and nodded. "Is better." She held it out toward me, then pulled it back again and fingered the fabric. "Is magick?"

"Yes. Or at least, it was," I said. "But I think the magick wore off, and—"

"Not wore off." The witch shook her head. "Just tired. I

fix." She flapped the cloak in the air a few more times, muttering words under her breath that I couldn't quite hear. At last, her expression satisfied, she held it out to me once again. "Now see."

I felt the magick before I even touched the now-clean and fully repaired fabric, a fine aura of energy that reached for my fingers just as I reached for the garment. Fixed was an understatement. I looked up at the witch. "How ...?"

"Magick bigger here in Uzzerworld." Baba Yaga shrugged and returned to her chair. "In Earse world, I am powerful witch. Here, I am more. Is why you stuck to ground."

Her words confirmed my earlier suspicions, and I nodded. I was glad I wasn't staying in the Otherworld. I didn't relish the idea of starting all over again the way I'd had to do when I first learned of my powers. Soon we would be in Odin's lands, and then after that—maybe, if we were lucky—

My thoughts screeched to a halt so suddenly that I gave a little *oof.* Oh hell. What if my magick didn't work as expected in Camlann, either? What if I got there and I had nothing to defend myself—or Lucan—with? What if—

"Sleep, little one," Baba Yaga said.

Sleep? Now? With that massive sinkhole of despair in my brain? I snorted to myself because it was not freaking likely, but I arranged the cloak over me and my companions as best I could without disturbing them. I might as well be warm while I imagined all the things that could—and likely would—go wrong.

Baba Yaga *tsked* as if she could hear my thoughts. "Sleep," she repeated.

And between the soft, familiar warmth of my cloak and the sway of the house as it strode through the mountains, I did.

CHAPTER 25

BABA YAGA FED US MORE STEW IN THE MORNING (SHE AND Keven would have gotten along famously), tucked a pouch of meat and another of ambrosia into my hand, and then deposited us at the edge of the forest that marked the start of Odin's land—me, Gus, and one dragon baby.

I made a last-ditch effort to un-adopt the latter, but my feeble objections landed on deaf ears, and before I knew it, we were watching the house stride back up into the mountains. Or at least, I was. The dragon baby chased something in the tall grass along the spider strand that Baba Yaga had assured me was the same as the one I'd previously followed, and Gus watched with the kind of disdain peculiar to cats.

I nudged the cat with my toe, and he twitched his tail in response. "You have only yourself to blame," I told him. "You're the one that ignored the Weaver and ran off to save him, remember? And speaking of him, he's going to need a name."

I regarded the fuzzy beast romping through the grass. What did one name a dragon, anyway? The obvious *Fluffy* sprang to mind, but he wouldn't remain fluffy forever, and I couldn't imagine calling something the size of his father—wait, was it even a boy?

I hadn't thought to ask Baba Yaga, and I had no idea how to tell. Not that it mattered, because Fluffy wouldn't work either way. But something similar? Its feathers resembled those of an ostrich, when I thought about it, and ostrich feathers were—

"Harry!" I exclaimed. Hairy, Harry—it worked. And if it turned out to be a girl, I could say that it was short for Harriet.

137

If anyone ever asked. Or met him/her. Or saw me again. Or—

"Harry," I repeated, turning my thoughts away from melancholy as the dragon rolled out of the grass and into Gus. "Your name is Harry."

Harry sneezed his agreement, and I dived down to pat out the flames on Gus's backside. The cat leveled a filthy look at both of us, then stood and picked his way along the strand leading through the woods, his every line one of offense. His dragon—because Harry was very much *his*, at least for the moment—tumbled happily after him, leaving me to bring up the rear.

The forest had become more heavily wooded as we walked, and trees towered on both sides of the strand, their silence brooding and oppressive. Even Harry's enthusiasm dwindled after a few minutes. He stopped bouncing and crept closer to Gus, following so close that the cat's tail brushed against his chest as it swished back and forth. Gus, in his turn, became tense with watchfulness rather than insult, stopping now and again to stare into the trees, his whiskers twitching. My nerves tightened with every stop he made, every snap of a twig beneath our feet. Was there something wrong, I wondered, or was this how Odin's land was all the time? Either way, I didn't like it. No wonder Baba Yaga had refused to take us further.

My unease grew, and I began to mull over our options. They were limited at best. Keep going and hope the witch was right, or turn back and—

Well. Perhaps nonexistent was a better word than limited.

A hollow thud beneath my foot signaled a change in the path, and a serious lapse in my attention. I stopped and blinked at the wooden bridge stretching before us—more of a boardwalk, really—that stretched across a lake. Beneath it, the waters were shallow, still, and clear, with stones and sand visible below their surface. The spider strand ran alongside it, and at the other end of both sat an island covered in tall pines and half shrouded in clouds that hung low in the sky. I shivered. The air here was far, far warmer than it had been on the frozen plateau, but it somehow managed to feel colder. Darker.

At my feet, Harry sneezed, and a stream of fire wrapped around a wooden rail. I reached to pat it out, but there was no need. The rail bore not so much as a scorch mark. We appeared to have found Odin's abode, all right—or at least the bridge to it. Which meant we'd made it. We'd crossed the god world and found the way into Camlann.

Almost.

I curled the fingers of my staff-less hand into my palm until my nails bit into the skin, then pulled back shoulders that had settled into wannabe defeat. Camlann—and Lucan—were on the other side of this, I reminded myself. Only Odin remained between me and them, and it wasn't like I hadn't dealt with a god or two before him. I could do this. I could absolutely do this.

I SO COULDN'T DO THIS.

I clutched at the rails on either side of me, my fingers so tight it was a wonder they didn't dent the wood. The moment both my feet had touched the bridge's surface, it had bucked beneath me, throwing me to my knees and sending Gus and Harry scrabbling not to fall into the water. Gus had rescued himself, but only my instinctive grab for blue fluff had saved Harry. The bridge had continued to heave, and I'd backed off, Harry in tow, to take stock of the situation.

It had boiled down to one thing: I was here, and I needed to be there—on the other side. Whether the bridge liked it or not, we were crossing. Ignoring Harry's squawks of protest, I'd stuffed the dragon into my rucksack, hoped to heaven he wouldn't set it and me on fire with one of his sneezes, and buckled it shut to keep him in there. And then, with my staff tucked under one arm and hanging onto the rails on each side for dear life, I'd inched my way across to where we were now, midpoint on a structure determined to pitch us into the lake. This time, my staff hadn't made it.

Just as I'd considered simply wading through the lake to the island, a particularly vicious twist of the boards had thrown me to my knees, and I'd lost my grip on my last link to Lucan. I'd grabbed for the staff but instinctively pulled my hand back as the dark shadow of something rippled beneath it. Then the bridge twisted again, and I'd staggered back to my feet, abandoning my attempts to retrieve the staff along with the idea of wading anywhere. If the bridge was this dangerous, I didn't want to encounter whatever the shadow was. And so we had persevered, until it was too far to go back and too far to continue, and—

The bridge bucked again and again, sloshing water over the edge and onto my boots and my bedraggled cat. My aching hands slipped a little in their grip, as exhausted as the rest of me. And now we were here, and I didn't know how much longer I could hold on. Or how much longer poor Gus could, for that matter, claws or no claws.

I did know that I wasn't going to make it to the other side.

I couldn't even see the other side anymore, I realized with a little jolt. The low clouds I'd noted on our arrival at the lake had enshrouded the island completely and were creeping toward us, and a glance over my shoulder found our starting point likewise obscured. It was as if the world around us had dissolved, and there was only me, Gus, Harry, and this damnable bridge.

"Fuck," I muttered as the bridge twisted in another direction.

Why the hell hadn't Freya warned me about this part?

Another heave beneath me, this one sharp enough to make my head snap back and forth, and—

"Enough!" I bellowed at it. "For goddess's sake, just *stop*."

And just like that, it did, leaving my voice to carry in an eerie echo out across the lake. *"Enough, ough, ough … stop, op, op …"*

I almost fell over at the abrupt cessation of movement, and I continued to hold on for long minutes, feet spread wide in waiting. But the wood stayed still. The ripples in the lake from its gyrations faded and the water's surface turned to glass again. The clouds stopped moving toward us.

Even Harry's thrashing in the rucksack on my back had stopped. Because he'd gone to sleep, or because he felt the change, too?

In the profound and utter silence that followed, a chill slithered along my skin. I had no idea why, but this felt as dangerous as the bridge's antics had. Maybe more so. A muffled thud reached my ears. Others followed. Steady, evenly spaced. *Thud, thud, thud, thud …*

I glanced at my right hand resting on the rail. A faint vibration accompanied the thudding, growing stronger as the sound drew nearer, and I strained my ears, trying to determine where it came from, ahead or behind. *Thud, thud* turned to *clop, clop*. A horse. A horse was approaching from … there. I strained to peer into the clouds that hid the island. A shadow moved in them, gradually becoming clearer.

Stooping, I scooped a wet, shivering Gus into my arms and tucked him inside my cloak, partly to keep him safe and partly for my own comfort. The further into this world I ventured, the more I valued his presence here with me. The gift of his companionship. If I ever made it back to Keven, she would get the most enormous hug from me for sending the cat along. Many hugs. *So* many hugs.

The shadow emerged abruptly from the clouds, became a massive black horse and armored rider, and stopped. I sucked in a breath and clutched Gus closer. Long moments dragged by. The horse pawed at the bridge with one foreleg and tossed its head with a snort, sending a cloud of steam into the air. The rider let go of the reins and lifted the helmet hiding his face.

Broad-shouldered and barrel-chested beneath his armor, he had untidy gray hair atop a face whose lines might have been chiseled from a glacier, so cold and unmoving were they, and his eyes were the same color and hardness as the steel of the sword he'd half drawn from its sheath at his waist. He stared across the dozen or so feet separating us.

"You are not her," he said at last.

"I—" I didn't know how to answer.

"You have her voice, but you are not her."

It had sounded like an observation the first time, but now it sounded like an accusation, and what the freaking hell did he mean, I had her voice?

My mouth flapped for a second while I searched for the right words—ones that would defuse the situation rather than get me beheaded.

"My name is Claire Emerson," I began—it was weak, but it was a start—"and I need to speak with—"

The sword came further out of its sheath. "Why do you have the voice of the Morrigan?"

Honestly, that goddess was going to be the literal death of me in this world. I tucked Gus under one arm and brought my other hand out from under my cloak in a placating gesture. "It's difficult to explain," I said. "But she sent me"— in a roundabout way, kind of—"to speak with Odin."

"Then you were a fool to heed her." Fully unsheathed now, the sword glinted menacingly in the pale light that filtered through the clouds.

My mouth twisted. "So I understood from Freya," I said, "but I—"

"Freya?" The name was sharp on his tongue but underscored by a hoarseness that made me think …

I swept back a stray hair that tickled my nose. "You're him. You're Odin, aren't you?"

The man sheathed the sword, replaced his helmet, and nudged his mount toward me. Then, before I could object—or react at all—he leaned down, grabbed my arm, and yarded me onto the horse behind him. The animal surged into a gallop, and out of sheer self-preservation, I released my hold on Gus and grabbed for the armored waist in front of me.

Claws sank into my shoulder as cat and I both clung on for dear life.

CHAPTER 26

THE TRIP ACROSS THE REMAINDER OF THE BRIDGE TO THE island was short. Blessedly so, because I couldn't have hung on for much longer and was in fact already hanging half off the horse when it skidded to a halt in front of a sprawling log structure. Gus detached himself from my shoulder in time to land on his feet, ears laid back. He wore his most ticked-off expression as I slid down into a heap beside him. Still astride the horse and ignoring me, Odin bellowed something at the building.

I got to my feet with as much grace as I could manage, which wasn't much with my cloak tangled around my legs and the rucksack hanging askew on my back. As I straightened both, grateful that Harry had remained quiet through all of this, I took a moment to check out the building. Whatever I might have imagined a god's residence to be, it hadn't been a log house. Well, more of a fancy lodge, really, because it somehow managed to be stately looking as well as rustic, but it was still a log house—and there, running past it and into the woods beyond, was the spider strand from the bridge.

I barely had enough time for a quick inhale before the lodge door opened and a woman built like a tank stepped onto the thick planks of the porch. Odin issued rapid-fire orders to her in a language I assumed was Norse. The woman nodded, eyeing me up and down with mixed curiosity and distrust. She stomped down the stairs, took my elbow in an iron grip, and frog-marched me toward the log building.

"Her name is Thyra," Odin called after me. "She does not speak your language. She will bring you to me when you are fit to be seated at my table."

I tried to pull my unwanted handmaid to a stop so that I

could tell Odin I didn't have time for such niceties, but it was like trying to stop the tank Thyra resembled. She didn't slow down, didn't miss a step, didn't seem to even notice my efforts. With her free hand, she pushed open a massive wooden door that looked to have been assembled from lashed-together tree trunks, and I marveled—no pun intended—at how very wrong the movies had gotten things.

Nothing about this world of gods was anything remotely like I'd expected. From the ruined landscape where I'd entered, to the waterfall chasm, to the frozen Yggdrasill surrounded by the towering mountains of stone and snow, and now the cloud-shrouded lake and island, the entire place felt —disjointed, and not just because of the varying landscapes. Perhaps because now I knew it to be held together by the Weaver's strands?

But Earth was held together by the same, and I had never sensed the same lack of cohesion there. Or maybe I'd never thought about it that way. Never had reason to.

Thyra dragged me down a hallway and into a room with a large, rectangular wooden box in the center of it. The floor, walls, and ceiling were likewise made of wood, but I noticed that only in passing. My mind was otherwise occupied.

Something else about the Otherworld bothered me— something I couldn't quite put my finger on. It didn't help my already-nebulous thought process to have Thyra's hands pushing me this way and that as she stripped my clothing from me. My rucksack went first, tossed into a corner and landing with a soft *whomp* that made me wince on Harry's behalf. I craned my neck to keep it in sight as Thyra tugged my sweater from my jeans. The rucksack sat without moving, and worry nagged at me. Surely Harry wouldn't have slept through that —was he okay? Had he somehow escaped?

I tried to remember whether the rucksack's weight had changed. Surely I would have noticed if it had. Then again, I'd been so focused on not being thrown from the bridge—and then staying on the horse—that maybe not. I uneasily pictured the dragon running around the wooden lodge, sneezing and setting fire to everything. It would serve Odin right but probably wouldn't help my cause much.

Thyra pulled the sweater over my head, and I lost sight of the rucksack. I reached to help with the clasp on my bra, but she rapped my fingers sharply, grumbled under her breath, and solved the garment dilemma by yanking it, too, straight up and over my head.

I yelped as it scraped over my breasts and caught on my nose. My "helper" muttered and rolled her eyes, obviously unimpressed with my show of weakness, and yanked at the waistband of my jeans.

Before I knew it, I was naked, seated in a tub of water cold enough to make me gasp, and having at least three layers of skin scrubbed from my body from head to toe. I tried to object, but my protests fell on deaf ears, and every attempt I made to take possession of the soap earned me a slap on the hand. I finally gave up and settled for enduring the ordeal. The sooner Thyra was satisfied, the sooner I could get dressed, get the vial Freya had given me from the rucksack, and drug Odin. And then, Camlann.

I was almost there.

I stole a peek at the rucksack, which still hadn't moved. Now I was really worried about Harry. I itched to go and check on him, but a sudden deluge of water poured over my head distracted me. I sputtered and flailed for the side of the tub. Thyra pushed my hand aside and soaped up my hair, then raked her fingers against my scalp to lather it. She was nothing if not thorough, and dear goddess, but she was strong. I hadn't been bathed—at least, not in this manner—by someone else since I was a child, and even then I didn't think it had ever been quite this painful.

Two more deluges washed over me, and then strong hands lifted me up and out of the tub and set me on the floor. I felt a towel touch my skin and grabbed for it, using a corner to wipe my face before Thyra tugged it away again and used it to dry my hair and remove my remaining skin. At last, she stood back, nodded satisfaction, and tossed the towel on top of the rucksack. Then she took a long, brown garment from a hook on the door and came at me again.

But I'd had enough of being manhandled, and I needed to check on Harry and get the vial Freya had given me before I met Odin again. The god had mentioned a table, which hopefully meant food, which I desperately needed, and wine, which might be my only chance to carry out Freya's instructions and get the hell out of here. I held up both hands against my unwanted maid's advance and scowled my best, fiercest scowl, because I had no intention of missing that chance.

In the end, with much gesticulating, I managed to convince Thyra that I could dress myself and that she didn't need to supervise. Frowning at me, she collected my dirty clothing from the floor, yanked open the door, and stepped out of the room, making a gesture I took to mean that I should hurry. I nodded agreement, and the door closed.

I wasted no time. I dropped the wooden bar across the door to secure it, slipped the dress over my head and slid my arms into the sleeves, ignored the laces that needed to be tightened to close the gaping front, and dived for the rucksack. Kneeling beside it, I dumped the contents unceremoniously on the floor—and then, in horror, stared first at the limp blue fuzz-ball that was my dragon, then at the empty glass vial rolling away from him.

Oh no, I thought. *No, no, no, no …*

And …

FUCK.

CHAPTER 27

A POUNDING AT THE DOOR ROUSED ME AFTER WHAT FELT LIKE an eternity but was likely only seconds, because Thyra wasn't the sort to wait an eternity. Her voice called through the wood to me, and while the words were indistinguishable, her tone was clear. I had about ten seconds before she broke down the entire door—a feat I had no doubt she was capable of.

"Coming," I croaked. Then I said it again, louder this time. "Coming."

Feverishly, I stuffed my belongings back into the rucksack, pausing to make sure that the fluffy little wretch that was Harry still breathed (he did) before adding him to the contents, too. The last item to go in was the empty vial. I clutched it in my fist for a moment, eyes closed—*Freaking hell, Harry, really? My one chance?*—and then I shoved it to the bottom of the bag. As I withdrew my hand, my fingers brushed against the Thor figurine that Braden had given me to keep me safe, and a part of me that may or may not have been a memory of Edie cackled in my brain.

Because, oh, the irony.

I secured the rucksack and stood, my knees stiff from the recent abuse inflicted on them, then slung the strap over my head and across my chest. The rucksack nestled in the small of my back, warm with Harry's heat. I sent up a quick prayer to whoever cared to listen that he would remain asleep, then lifted the bar from the door and opened it.

Thyra eyed me narrowly as I laced up the front of the dress, and her suspicious gaze went past me to scan the room. She grunted something, then motioned for me to take off the rucksack. I shook my head.

"No," I said. "I'm keeping it."

She made to lift the strap, but I stepped out of reach, tightening my lips. I shook my head again, and she rolled her eyes. With another mutter, she flapped her hands in a *whatever* gesture, then turned and stomped down the corridor, back the way we'd come. Assuming I was supposed to follow, I fell into step behind her.

ODIN WAS SEATED AT THE HEAD OF A MASSIVE WOODEN TABLE in a windowless dining room. Torches burned in sconces along opposite log walls, their smoke hanging in a thin haze over the table. Mounted heads and skins of animals—bear, deer, moose, and some I didn't recognize—were displayed between them. And on the wall behind Odin, the head of a dragon held pride of place.

I shifted the rucksack strap on my shoulder and silently begged Harry to stay drugged.

Odin looked up from feeding my cat, bless his nine lives, who was seated on the table beside him, clean, dry, and daintily accepting the offered tidbits. The god nodded satisfaction, presumably at my improved appearance.

"Sit," he commanded, pointing a few places away from him. There, a man who looked more like he should be commanding a Viking ship than butlering stood by a drawn-out chair. "Eat. We will talk."

I moved to do as I was told, my mind still racing after the discovery of the empty vial. I'd considered and discarded so many ideas that my brain spun—and I still had no solution as to how to get out of my predicament. So, with no recourse, I took off the rucksack and set it and Harry on the floor at my feet, and sat at a table with a god who'd been dumped by the goddess who had given me half her powers, and ate a delicious venison steak and roasted vegetables, and drank a dark red wine more potent than any I'd ever had before and—

Odin pushed away his plate. "Now, we talk," he announced.

Within seconds, the Viking cleared away the remains of the meal and disappeared through a doorway, balancing platters and plates with a graceful aplomb very much at odds with his appearance. Odin waited until the door closed behind him, then leaned forward. He placed his elbows on the table, steepled his fingers, and stared directly into my unease.

"Tell me about the Morrigan," he said. "And about my wife."

Once again, I found myself telling my story about the war between the Crones and Morok, and the transfer of half of the Morrigan's power into me; about the splintering of the Earth world and the portal to Camlann that had been opened in my final battle with Morok. But I shared less with him than I had with Freya. Where I had sensed a softening in her demeanor as I spoke, Odin gave me no such impression, and after Freya's warning, I was under no illusion that I might make an ally of him.

He needed enough to convince him to let me go and let me pass, and that was all.

"So you have been successful in stopping him, then," Odin said.

"Not ... exactly."

"How do you mean?"

I sighed, choosing my words as carefully as I might my steps across a minefield. "We think he still lives—in the splinter of Camlann, where all of this started—and that he will try to return."

"And this Camlann is where?"

"The Weaver—"

"You've spoken to the Weaver of All?"

I nodded. "When I came through the doorway from

Earth. She showed me the strand that I'm supposed to follow."

He snorted. "Let me guess. It led you here."

"Yes, and it passes through your lands. Camlann is at the end of it." I hoped.

"I see." He lounged in his chair, one arm slung over the back, the other resting on the table, thumb rubbing lightly over his fingertips as he watched me and waited.

"I need—" I stopped at the glint of hardness that returned to his gaze, then rephrased. "Respectfully," I said, "I request permission to continue to follow the Weaver's strand. To cross your lands to Camlann."

"You haven't told me about Freya yet."

"I—what?" The sudden change of topic startled me.

"My *wife*. Where did you meet her?"

"By Yggdrasill. I underestimated the cold of the plateau, and she found me there, nearly frozen. She saved my life."

"Did she not recognize you as the Morrigan?"

"She told me I stank of crows," I admitted, and the god across the table threw back his head in a great shout of laughter that rang through the room.

"I can imagine she did," he said. "There is little love lost between Freya and the Morrigan."

I bit down on the *"Is it any wonder?"* hovering on the end of my tongue and instead made a noncommittal murmur.

"Why did she not bring you here herself?" he asked. "It would have made everything much simpler."

"For me, yes," I said. His eyes narrowed, and it was plain that he understood the double meaning behind my words. I kept my gaze level and my expression bland, however, and after a moment, he grunted.

"Yes. Well. Returning to your request, what is in it for me?"

My heart dropped to sit beside the rucksack on the floor. This was it. This was where I decided between the option

Freya had said I should under no circumstances accept, and the one where I attempted my very unpredictable magick again.

As options went, neither was great, but at least promising Odin a favor afforded me the possibility of actually making it to Camlann. My magick, on the other hand, might well result in another catastrophe that would end my trip here—because I didn't think Odin would be as willing to rescue me as Freya and Baba Yaga had been. Or as understanding. At my feet, the rucksack shifted, signaling Harry's return to the land of the conscious, and my gaze flicked to the dragon's head mounted on the wall behind Odin.

Beneath the table, I crossed the index and middle fingers on my right hand in the ages-old gesture used by those about to lie—or to make a promise they had no intention of keeping. Then I met the steel-cold gaze of the god of war.

"What would you like?" I asked.

My path was chosen.

CHAPTER 28

An unspecified favor.

As I trudged down the path Thyra had set us on, I could find nothing good in the promise I'd made to Odin, and I was pretty sure Freya would agree. No matter how I framed it, not knowing what the god would demand—or when he would demand it—was unsettling in the extreme. And I didn't think my childish crossed fingers would hold much sway with him when he came to collect.

My only consolation lay in knowing what he didn't—that if I did make it to Camlann, I didn't expect to return, and he would likely never have the chance to collect on my promise. And making it to Camlann remained a big *if*.

The moment my promise of a favor had crossed my lips, my tenuous welcome had come to an abrupt end. Odin had shoved back his chair and bellowed for Thyra. There had been no offer of help in crossing his land, no packages of food, no small kindness of any sort. I'd barely had time to grab my rucksack and clean but wet clothing from her with one hand and my cat—drowsy with a full belly—with the other before the tank had shoved me out the door and into the clammy fog that had settled over the island. More shoves had taken me to the edge of the woods beside the log house, where Thyra had pointed a finger at an opening in the trees, her face daring me to disagree with her.

I hadn't. Even in the gloom cast by clouds and fog, I'd been able to make out the Weaver's strand disappearing into the trees with the path, and a glance in the direction it came from confirmed that it seemed to be the one from the bridge. Seemed to. I had no idea if it really was, or even if we still followed the right strand. I'd relied on Freya to show me the way once, Baba Yaga after that, and now Odin. Any—or all—of them might have been wrong, and I would never know.

Well. I might eventually figure it out when I died in this godforsaken world without reaching Camlann, but—

A part of me that sounded like Edie had snorted at the idea that the god world could be *godforsaken* and, for a moment, joy had sparked in me. Then I'd remembered that it was only Edie's echo and, when Thyra had grunted and pointed again, I'd obediently started down the path, because there was nothing else I could do. That, and I was more than happy to put her and Odin behind me.

I shifted Gus from my left arm to my right and hefted him partway onto my shoulder. We'd been walking for about an hour now, and the cat was no lightweight. I'd tried setting him down a couple of times, but every time I did, he parked his furry butt in the middle of the path and commenced bathing himself, and Harry refused to leave his side. I'd be damned if I was going to leave either of them behind after what we'd gone through to get here, and so I carried him while Harry bounced down the path ahead of us.

Thankfully, the dragon had remained drowsy enough to stay quiet until we were clear of the house and Thyra's suspicious eyes, but he was well rested now and, dear goddess, he had a lot of energy after his prolonged nap. For the first while, I'd kept a close eye on him, afraid that he would wander off in pursuit of something, but it seemed that baby dragons stuck close to their *muzzers*. He showed no inclination to be more than a few feet away from his adopted one, which freed me up to think about other things.

So many other things.

I missed my staff. I missed my family. I missed my friends. I wondered what lay ahead in Camlann. What a splinter of our world would look like. How I would find Morgana's magick. How I would find Lucan. What or who I would look for first, or whether Morok would find me before I found either and make all of the preceding moot.

I wondered if I had it in me to fight him again.

I tried not to dwell on the latter, but it was the proverbial elephant in the room and pretty hard to ignore. This trip across the Otherworld had taken more out of me than I would have liked and, as Edie had once said, I didn't bounce as well as I used to when I was young.

A subtle but undeniable ache had settled into every bone, every joint, every *every*. I was tired, I hurt, and, dear goddess, but I didn't want to be here—or in Camlann, or facing Morok again, or ...

I realized I had tears trickling down my cheeks, and I stopped walking to wipe my face with the edge of my cloak. *Stop wallowing*, I told myself fiercely. *You don't have time for a pity party.*

I was unconvinced, however, because seriously, why me? Why should a sixty-year-old grandmother, who at one time hadn't even been able to keep track of a pair of glasses, be tasked with going to battle with a god—for a second time, no less—in order to save the entire world?

I scowled at the question, because the answer was that I shouldn't be. I shouldn't be wielding half the power of a goddess, I shouldn't be traipsing across the Otherworld in search of a splinter of our world or hidden magick or a wolf-shifter, and—and, freaking hell, I shouldn't even *know* about any of it.

Gus struggled in my grip, interrupting my internal grumping, and I let him drop to the ground. He landed with a soft thump on the pine needle-covered path, drawing Harry's attention. The little dragon chirped with joy and hurled himself at the cat, who batted him aside, hissed, and set about finally giving himself the bath he wanted. Harry—with a great deal more respect this time—crept up carefully and snuggled into the cat's side. A flick of Gus's ears said that he noticed, but the dragon was allowed to stay, and I found a smile curving my lips despite my circumstances.

I closed my eyes, tipped my head back, drew a deep breath in through my nose, held it, and released it in a long, measured sigh. Then I drew another and did the same. Then a third. When the last of the third exhale left my lungs, I opened my eyes again and let my chin drop to where it belonged. Then I looked around me, at the towering trees, at the spider strand, at the cat washing himself while the adopted fuzz ball snuggled up to his side, and at the empty path forward and the equally empty one behind us. And then it hit me.

Why me?

Quite simply because there was no one else.

CHAPTER 29

ONCE AGAIN, I HAD NO WAY TO GAUGE HOW LONG WE WALKED. Like the first part of the Otherworld that Gus and I had landed in, there seemed to be no delineation between night and day here. Unlike the first part, which had existed in a steady brightness, Odin's lands seemed to live in perpetual gloom. It was more than a bit oppressive.

Not unlike the god who ruled over it, I suspected.

I tried—and failed—to picture him and the Morrigan together. Or the Morrigan and Morok, for that matter. How, I wondered, did one make love to a goddess who kept dissolving into a flock of crows? The image of Odin scowling as he tried to hold onto a raucously cawing murder made me laugh; but one of Morok made me shiver, because I could see nothing more than a shadow where he should have been. I'd only ever seen him in Kate's form—had he retained that when he went through the portal? Or had the magick stripped him of her body and returned him to his?

It was a sobering thought, because if it were the latter and there were still other people in Camlann, I had no way to recognize him.

Without warning, Gus darted off the trail ahead of me and into the trees on the left. My heart skipped a beat and I instinctively dropped into a crouch. My right hand snapped shut—but this time on empty air, rather than the staff that I had always carried. Loss slammed into me yet again. I shoved it away and dived to scoop up Harry before he could follow the cat. Whatever was out there, Gus at least had a chance of avoiding it. The baby dragon did not.

Harry let out an indignant squawk, and I tried to find his muzzle in amongst the fuzz.

"Hush," I hissed at him, but there was no need. Gus was already back, his jaws clamped around a black rodent whose tail thrashed wildly. A rat. With a shudder, I released the wriggling Harry and turned away as the little dragon attacked his adopted mother's offering with glee. The rat emitted a single, high-pitched, ear-piercing shriek and then went silent. Harry, not so much.

Soft snarls and grunts of pleasure intermingled with the crunch of bones, and I tried not to picture the carnage taking place. To distract myself, I began setting up a camp of sorts—heavy on the *of sorts*, given how little I carried. I might not have known how long we'd been walking, but I knew it had been enough for one day.

I spread my cloak on the ground and dumped the contents of the rucksack onto it. There was precious little. During his time of confinement, Harry had torn open the packages of food that Baba Yaga had given me. The meat was gone, but the ambrosia was still there—albeit in a somewhat questionable state. I picked a blue feather out of the open package and grimaced. Perhaps later, if I got hungry enough? I set it aside and looked down with another grimace at the clothing Thyra had stripped from me.

I'd hoped to change out of the ridiculous dress she had given me to wear, but jeans and sweater alike were still wet from our adventure on Odin's bridge, and I had no intention of trying to dry them with magick after the Yggdrasill incident. Once burned, twice shy, so to speak.

I heard a small sneeze behind me and looked around in time to see the end of Gus's tail catch fire. Before the cat could react, I slapped my hand over the flames to snuff them out, earning myself a hiss in exchange.

"You're welcome, you ungrateful feline," I said. Then I looked at Harry, who was turning in circles, seeking a comfortable curling-up place. "I don't suppose you could do that on purpose, could you? Maybe light me a fire to dry out my clothes?"

The dragon settled into a ball, his bloodstained snout tucked under his tail. Within seconds, a vibrating noise rose from him. Yup. He'd definitely learned how to purr. And no, I wasn't going to get a fire. So be it.

I hung the jeans over the branch of one tree, sweater over another, and bra and underwear beside the latter, and hoped for the best. Then I wrapped myself in my cloak, grateful that it, at least, was dry thanks to the magick Baba Yaga had restored to it. Finally, with the empty rucksack as a pillow, I settled onto the pine-needle path and fell into an instant, dreamless sleep.

IN THE MORNING—OR AFTERNOON OR EVENING OR WHATEVER time of day it was—I salvaged a little of the ambrosia for my breakfast while Gus and Harry shared another rat that Gus had caught. It wasn't enough for either of them, but they both seemed content enough, and I felt a certain pride in how well my cat had adapted to his role as caregiver. He'd even deigned to wash Harry's face in the aftermath of their meal.

Their developing connection was a bright spot in this otherwise decidedly not-bright land of Odin's, and it made me glad that we'd brought the dragon along. I liked the idea that Gus would at least have someone else to keep him company if anything happened to—

Well. So much for a bright spot.

I snuffed out a fire started by Harry in the dry pine needles on the path, then tucked the remaining ambrosia back into its package and into the rucksack. Standing up, I stripped off the dress and slithered and tugged my way into my still-damp clothing, gritting my teeth at the cold clamminess. Then I shook out the cloak and swung it around my shoulders, picked up the rucksack, and turned to my companions.

"Right," I said. "Let's go find Camlann, shall we?"

Gus yawned and stretched, shook himself, and headed down the path with Harry chirping and tumbling after him. I brought up the rear, happy to follow the two small animals and watch the dragon's antics. Happier still to find the stiffness in my hips and back easing as I walked. My strides lengthened. I took a deep, lung-expanding breath. I—

I blinked. Froze mid-step. Stared in slack-jawed disbelief.

A dozen feet ahead of me, Gus and Harry trotted on and, before I could recover enough to yell at them to stop, disappeared into what seemed like thin air. Seemed like but wasn't, because we'd done it. We'd found the door.

It took several long seconds for my brain to process the realization. Several more to argue with itself, because how could I have not noticed the distinct magick glow that it emitted? It was obvious now that the path ended in a wall of sparkles and energy—but where was its protector? Surely, it couldn't be this easy. What, we just walked up to it and … through? No.

But yes. Because that's exactly what Gus and Harry had just done.

I just didn't believe it. Couldn't believe it.

Didn't *want* to believe it.

I realized I was trembling from head to toe so hard that my teeth chattered. That was the crux of it, wasn't it? I didn't want to believe that we'd made it, that I'd found the doorway into Camlann, because that meant I'd found Camlann itself, and as old and tired and horribly unprepared as I felt, now I was going to have to step through and into the splinter. I was going to have to step up.

Fuck, I thought hazily. *Fuckity, fuck, fuck* …

A screeching blue fuzz-ball flew out of the doorway and into my arms, landing with a *whomp* against my chest that knocked the wind out of me.

CHAPTER 30

HARRY'S PANICKED RETURN CHANGED EVERYTHING. OR, rather, the fact that Gus didn't follow him changed everything. My cat needed me.

Forgetting my reservations and shoving aside my fears, I stuffed the dragon headfirst into the rucksack, slung it over my back, took a deep breath, and ran at the doorway.

I'd expected it would be like the first—a wall of semi-set gelatin that resisted my presence and robbed me of air. It wasn't.

This door was like a filmy curtain of cobwebs that parted the second I touched it, and so rather than fighting for my every step, my every breath, I sprawled headfirst on hard, rocky ground with my chin resting on what felt like a fur-covered stone. Except this stone moved.

I started to roll onto my back, remembered Harry, and pushed up instead onto my hands and knees. Tipping my head back, I stared my way up a granite leg, patchy with sparse fur. My heart sank with every inch of carved muscle that my gaze traveled, and I knew what I faced long before I reached the elongated face with the dog-like muzzle and beady eyes.

The goliath. The fucking goliath.

Of course that would be my first encounter here.

And there, clutched in its boulder-sized fist, was Gus. Adrenaline exploded in my chest. Fear and agony sucked it back in again. *Gus*, my mind whimpered. *My brave, beautiful—*

Impossibly, the ginger cat turned his head as if he'd heard me, and he yowled in a plaintive voice as he struggled to wriggle free. Another jolt of adrenaline hit my heart, this one causing a squeeze of physical pain.

"One more reason saving the world should be left to the young ones," I imagined Edie would say. She wouldn't be wrong.

I wrenched my attention away from the cat and focused on the goliath that swayed back and forth above me. If it had wanted to kill Gus, it would have squished the life out of him by now, I told myself. The fact that it hadn't meant something. It had to mean something.

At the very least, it meant I had a chance.

Carefully, slowly, I got to my feet and held my hands out to my sides, palms open, in what I hoped the goliath would see as a non-threatening pose. Its beady eyes shifted from one of my hands to the other, then back to meet my gaze. So far, so good. I took a steadying breath.

"My name is Claire," I began.

The goliath put its head back and roared. The sound shuddered through me and echoed in my memories, a hoarse, raw bellow that seemed to go on forever before it died into labored panting and the goliath looked at me again. I swallowed hard, trying not to notice that Gus had gone still.

"I know you," I said. "We've met before, remember? You were supposed to fight me then, but things are different here. I'm not your enemy. I don't want to hurt you, and I don't think you want to—"

The goliath snarled, and its back-and-forth sway intensified. My hands shook at my sides. Harry bounced around in the rucksack on my back. *Magick,* my mind whispered, but there was a hysterical edge to the thought that made me pause. I didn't know if—or how—my magick would work here in the splinter, but I did know that extreme emotion on my part had never been my friend in wielding it. I couldn't risk it. Not here. Not now. Not even for my Gus.

But I could try again to reach the goliath.

I drew myself up as tall as I could. Drew on the calm I had learned was at my center. Drew on everything I knew in myself that was not magick but was still power. Harry's thrashing stilled, as if he sensed the gravity of the negotiations taking place. And then I uttered a single, quiet word, believing with my entire being that the goliath was capable of hearing it, because it needed to be true.

"Please," I said.

For immeasurable seconds ... minutes ... eons, the goliath's gaze remained locked with mine before it tipped back its head to roar again. A scream this time. Guttural and unbearably mournful as I had heard it once before. Filled with a pain that wrapped around my heart and speared me to the core. Then, with the echo still rolling across the landscape, it opened its fist, let Gus drop to the ground in front of me, and turned to go.

Shock held me immobile for a split second, and then I dropped to my knees on the hard ground and grabbed the cat, ignoring his protests as I held him close. I'd done it. I'd convinced the goliath to release him, and—I sucked in a shuddering breath and burst into tears as the terror I'd held back swamped me at last. Fucking, fucking hell. I didn't know what I would have done if I hadn't—if I had—

I buried my face against the cat's side, crying into his fur. I couldn't bear to think about what might have happened. I'd never felt so alone. And terrified. Did I mention terrified? I leaned back and sideways until I thudded onto one hip, then my butt. Crossing my legs, I wrapped the cat closer still and cried harder.

I cried for all the times I'd come close to losing my cat, and for the times I'd nearly died myself. I cried for all the people I'd had to leave behind and the ones who had left me behind. I cried for a world that had no idea that it relied on tired, scared-to-death me to save it. I cried for how unutterably, completely, bone-deep weary I was, and how I would never know peace or comfort again, and for the multitude of gifts in my life that I had failed to truly notice until they were gone ... and for which it was now too late to be grateful.

The warmth of my son's hug. The softness of Braden's lips pressed to my cheek in a kiss. The feel of the sun on my face on a spring day. The scent of rain. The tart sweetness of summer's first strawberry. The hushed frozen beauty that followed a snowfall.

The miracle that was a cloud, a bird, a single blade of grass.

The goliath screamed in the distance, and I cried for it, too.

I cried, and cried, and cried some more, until my tears dried up and only heaving spasms remained, wracking me from head to toe, from body to soul. Until, at last, my breathing slowed and steadied, and with a final, deep, shaking breath, I was able to unlock my arms and set Gus on the ground.

As the cat shook himself off and licked a few hairs into place, I wiped the last of the tears from my face and used the bottom corner of my cloak to blow my nose, wondering whether Baba Yaga had refreshed its magick enough to deal with my slime, deciding I was too fucking tired to care.

Only then did I remember poor Harry. I slipped the rucksack off and turned the dragon free. While he and Gus enjoyed their joyous reunion—admittedly more joyous on Harry's part—I unwrapped and ate the last of the ambrosia. I'd meant it to last longer, but I hadn't counted on dehydrating myself with a crying jag. Goddess, but I needed to find water soon. I wondered if the goliath needed water, too. If following it—at a safe distance, of course—would be worth a try, or if I should go in the opposite—

I paused my thoughts. Cycled back on them. Groaned to myself. Despite my rather epic pity party, it seemed I wasn't quite ready to give up just yet. My pragmatism was already surfacing. With plans, questions, ideas. I considered trying to ignore it but had to admit that the alternative of simply lying there until I expired wasn't that appealing. I wouldn't be able to stand the boredom, for one.

I'd never been much good at doing nothing.

So, as Gus pinned Harry to the ground and subjected him to a thorough bathing, I pulled up my figurative socks, climbed to my feet to take stock of our surroundings—and then, in the same movement, sank to my knees again as utter, horrified disbelief slammed into me.

We'd found Camlann, all right. And the battlefield to prove it.

Somewhere on the other side of the blood-soaked plain, the goliath screamed.

CHAPTER 31

I PICKED MY WAY THROUGH WHAT HAD BEEN THE LAST
battlefield upon which King Arthur had fought—and by all
accounts died—alongside hundreds of others. Whether
Arthur's body still lay here, I didn't know. But other
bodies did.

Men and horses were strewn about on grass trampled flat
and earth stained dark with blood, piled on top of one
another with weapons in hand and wounds still gaping, faces
contorted in rage, agony, and the screams that had died with
them.

The carnage was spread across the grassland as far as the
eye could see, perfectly, eternally preserved. Exactly as it had
happened when the Morrigan had split Camlann from the
rest of the world.

Including the stench that permeated the air.

I clamped one hand over my nose to keep out the smell of
death, but the effort was futile. The coppery scent of blood,
mingled with that of voided bowels and bladders, hung in a
noxious, invisible cloud over the field that was so thick that I
could taste it. And I hadn't even reached the center yet.

The sheer volume of bodies slowed my progress. I wanted
to look away, to focus on the treeline on the other side of the
field and the tower on the hill rising beyond it, but I couldn't
move more than a foot in any direction without encountering
body parts—some attached, some not. To avoid stepping on
them, I had to keep looking. To keep seeing the faces. The
animals, the men, the boys—children, really—and, here and
there, a woman.

And everywhere, evidence of the wolves that Merlin,

possessed by Morok, had made of Arthur's soldiers and the gargoyles that Morgana, owned by the Morrigan, had brought to life to fight them. The gargoyle Morgana had herself become.

I tried not to tread on bloody soil or grass, either, but soon gave up on that because there was simply too much of it. Likewise, I gave up on keeping the bottom of my cloak clear of it, and I could feel its increasingly sodden weight dragging at my ankles, at my heart, at my soul.

So much death.

So much.

Even Gus and Harry seemed affected by it. They flanked me, silently weaving around the bodies as I did, careful not to step on one. Gus slunk along in the way cats do when nervous or unhappy, and Harry's steps held none of his usual bounce or enthusiasm. I considered putting the little guy back into the rucksack, but that would have meant stopping in the midst of the slaughter. Remaining beside one of the fallen. Feeling their sightless gaze tugging at the life in me.

Harry was on his own.

As slow as our progress was, we eventually reached the treeline, and I sagged with relief against a giant oak. Every inch of my skin crawled with remnants of death that seemed to cling to me, and it was all I could do not to rip my clothes off and burn them, cloak included. I frowned. Wait … not all of the crawling skin was due to the carnage we'd traversed. There was something else. Something—

I pulled away from the tree and stared at it. That. Something was wrong with that. I stood back to look up at it. It looked perfectly normal, just like an oak tree should. A solid trunk, strong branches, wide canopy of leaves, but—I stepped up to it again and traced the fingers of one hand down its bark—and then I knew.

It wasn't a tree. Not a whole one. It was … a sliver of a

tree. An image that had been peeled away from its original, which still existed—or at least had at one time—in the remainder of Earth. Just as Camlann had still existed, enough so that remnants of it had been dug up by archeologists and its stories had been passed along through the millennia. But as complete as it looked, the tree was missing a vital element.

It didn't live.

Jesus goddess. This entire place was dead, not just the beings who had lived here. Everything. Every tree, every blade of grass, every flower ... everything.

Which raised the question of how a place that had no life of its own could support a life that came into it. Or what would happen if it couldn't.

I liked neither the answers that whispered themselves to me nor the sudden shortening of my timeline that came with them. I needed to move. I needed to find Lucan if he still lived, to find the magick, and to find Morok—all before my own life became forfeit simply because I existed.

But first, I needed to do something about my cloak. Unable to stand the feel of it clinging to me any longer—it was wet up to my knees, now—I stripped it off and stuck it into the rucksack. I would rather have abandoned it altogether, but if my journey across the Otherworld had taught me anything, it was that resources were precious. Even the contaminated ones.

Something soft bumped against my shin, and I looked down into Harry's glittering blue eyes, more of an aquamarine now than the sapphire they'd been when we'd acquired him. And he was taller, too, I realized with a start. Our little dragon was growing up. He would need more food soon. Hell, he'd need food, period, considering the last meal he'd had was the rat he and Gus had shared.

We would all need food. And water. I turned to survey the woods. A wide path had been cut through the trees here, leading back toward the hill I'd seen. A hill that some historians in my distant, present-day world believed was the site of Camelot itself, which would mean a castle—and, more importantly, houses and shops and the possibility of surviving.

I hoped they were right.

IF THE BATTLEFIELD OF CAMLANN HAD BEEN NOTHING LIKE I'D imagined it, neither was Camelot when we reached it.

I stopped at the edge of the wide ditch that separated us from the wooden wall and the massive gates hung askew from it. At least fifteen feet high, one gate was half torn from its hinges and the other had been smashed into splinters, as if something had burst through from the other side. The opening they had once protected was empty, and the silence I sensed beyond them was utter. Complete.

And eerie as fuck.

I stared across the remains of the plank bridge separating us from the bailey and castle of legend. I did *not* want to go in there. I didn't think I would survive another scenario like the battlefield, and that smashed gate …

I shivered and rubbed one hand over the opposite arm. I didn't want to, but neither did I have much choice. We still needed food and water, and we were far more likely to find them inside those walls than we were out here.

Of course, we were also likely to find Morok there as well —but, again, not much choice. We would have to take our chances. I dropped my hand back to my side and called to the cat and dragon poking about in the underbrush. Together, we started across the plank bridge.

To my undying relief, it was a lot less bloody inside than I'd expected. But the eeriness remained.

I stood for long minutes inside the gates, my gaze scanning

what had once been a bustling barracks area. Ahead and to my left stood a huge open-walled structure with tables of turnips, potatoes, and cabbages in various stages of preparation, and trussed, still-feathered chickens hanging from the beams overhead. Benches were drawn up to the tables, and stone ovens and fire pits stood behind, some with pots hung over them by the people tasked with feeding the troops.

Women, children, men too old or damaged to fight, all of them trying to provide for their soldiers and to keep the fires burning on the hearths so their men—their fathers and sons and husbands—would have homes to return to.

To my right, stables and barns, with corrals that held sheep and cows and goats and …

And they had all dropped in place. Children clutching the sticks they'd been playing with. Old men beside the stumps and rough-hewn stools they'd been sitting on. Women with babes in arms. The Morrigan's magick had stripped the life from them and left only the shells, like three-dimensional cardboard cutouts forever locked in the moment when they had ceased. Unless …

I thought about the tree that had been a sliver of its original, an image peeled away and frozen here, the way Camlann itself had. Was it possible that the same had happened to the inhabitants? Would they have continued living in the Earth this had been taken from—*could* they have?

It didn't seem possible, but none of what I'd lived through over the last weeks had been possible. Not gods and goddesses, not creatures of the ether, not portals to splinters or doorways to the Otherworld …

Fuck it, I thought wearily. Trying to sort real from unreal was making my brain hurt and distracting me from what I needed to be doing. Possible or not, I was going with my image theory, if only because it was the least horrific option. Because there was already enough death on that battlefield.

But whether these people were dead or not, walking

among them was creepy as hell. Nothing moved. Not so much as a breeze stirred, there were no birds, nothing. Even Harry was so quiet that the only sounds were my footsteps, and I found myself tiptoeing in an effort to muffle those, too, as if I might disturb those who had fallen around me.

And then a wolf howled.

CHAPTER 32

MY STEPS FALTERED AND MY CHIN SNAPPED UP AS THE HOWL rose and fell, at once blood chilling and mournful—and close. I looked one way and then the other, trying to locate the source, but too soon, the sound died into silence. It didn't come again. Hope and dread tangled in my chest with the breath I held. Had I imagined it? Was I that desperate?

I exhaled in a rush. Perhaps the latter was true, but the way Harry pressed in against a ridge-backed Gus told me that the howl had been real. Hope surged to the forefront. Lucan was here. He was alive. But where?

A cluster of ramshackle huts behind the open kitchen drew my gaze. The barracks.

I moved slowly, stopping to listen every few steps and to peer into doorways as I went. Doorways that revealed more cardboard cutouts of people, more slices of the lives that had once been at the center of Camelot's bailey. And then, in the second-last hut, as despair and doubt began to creep in, I found him.

No. I found what was left of him.

The wolf sat chained to the far wall, pressed up against the wood. His head hung low on thin shoulders, and his eyes were closed. His ribs heaved with each laborious breath, sticking out prominently beneath the formerly thick, tawny fur that was now caked with blood and filth. A tongue thick from lack of water protruded between his teeth. Horror gripped me. Permeated me. Became me.

I shook my head back and forth in silent denial of the creature I saw before me. No. No, no, no. This couldn't possibly be him. This couldn't be the proud, strong, nearly invincible protector I had known, whose friendship I had cherished.

It couldn't be … but I had no doubt that it was.

"Lucan," I whispered.

And then I jumped back, slapping a hand over my mouth to smother my scream as Lucan's head snapped around. Crazed amber eyes locked on me and his wolf launched itself at me with a snarl.

Harry screeched an alarm at my feet and fell backward out of the hut, Gus scrambling in his wake. Self-preservation dictated that I follow, too, but gut-wrenching despair rooted me to the floor. He didn't recognize me. Lucan didn't recognize me. And if he hadn't been chained to that wall, he would have already killed me.

I stared at him in shock, trying to convince myself that I was wrong, that he was only surprised by my appearance—that he would calm down when he realized …

But he didn't. If anything, his wolf's attempts to get at me became more and more frenzied, more rage-fueled. I felt for the door frame and sagged against it.

Now what? Slowly, I slid down to the floor, wrapped my arms around my knees, and watched the snarling, slavering wolf throwing himself against the end of the chain holding him. I had nothing. No idea what to do next, or where to go, or—

A slow anger began to burn in my belly. It kindled into fury and loathing, and then into the first true hatred I'd ever felt in my life. Morok had done this. I could feel the magick emanating from Lucan—no, not from Lucan, but from the collar that encircled his neck. I probed further, and hatred became loathing as I began to understand just what the god had done.

The collar's magick held Lucan in his wolf form and made shifting or escape impossible. It made sure he would suffer as long as possible while he wasted away without food or—

I looked away from the wolf to search the space around him. Nope. Not so much as a bowl of water. The little one-roomed hut held nothing except ...

My gaze swept the space a second time, then a third. Slowly, systematically, I made my eyes stop at each item and my brain catalog what I saw. A washstand with a metal pitcher and bowl. A table with three chairs. A row of pegs on the wall beside me that held a man's coat, a woman's cape, a small child's sweater. A double bed with a tiny cot beside it. And ...

And oh, dear goddess.

My gaze settled on the floor by the bed. On the bodies of a woman and child that lay there. On the only things that lay within a wolf's reach.

In a flash of understanding, a terrible, awful, horrific flash, I saw what Morok had done. Knew what the sadistic son of a ... no, the *fucker* had intended. He had tied Lucan up with no food or water, bound him to wolf form and removed his ability to be human, and then he had put the shifter's own wife and son beside him.

Agony rose from my toes, gathered in my chest, and emerged in a ragged half-groan, half-wail. On the other side of the little hut splintered by time and magick and misery, as if arrested by the sound, Lucan the wolf abruptly stopped fighting his restraints. He stared at me, and a shadow of awareness flared in the amber eyes. Anguish followed it.

As my wail slipped into silence, he tipped back his head and howled.

I should have gone looking for Morok, but I didn't.

I couldn't, not even knowing what was at stake. Because

with Lucan tied here, with what the dark god had done to him, I could focus on nothing more than salvaging whatever might be left of the man inside the wolf.

Twice, I tried to walk away on that first day. Twice, I fell to my knees in the dirt outside the hut, unable to see past my rage or feel past my agony at what I was leaving behind. After the second time, I knew I needed to see to my friend first and the world after. The survival of my very soul gave me no other choice.

It took two days (by my sleep calculations) and the remains of four chickens and half a goat to get past Lucan the wolf long enough to reach the man. He devoured the chickens in their entirety. I was careful to offer them one at a time with hours between so that I didn't make him sick, but it wasn't easy when I wanted nothing more than to ease his pain and see him return to the shifter I knew him to be. And to move the temptation of the woman and child out of his reach.

At last, while he was busy on the second day with the goat I'd hacked apart for him, I crawled cautiously across the floor to the woman and, seizing her by the ankles, dragged her body back toward the door with me. Her arms were locked around the child, so blessedly, he came with us, out of reach of his father—but not before Lucan finished his meal.

I stopped moving and held my breath for a moment when his soft snarl reached my ears, but the wolf didn't try to stop us—me—and so I pulled some more, until we were clear of him. Until they were safe. Only then did I let myself look, really look, upon my protector's family—to see what damage he might have done to them, to see who they had been.

She had been young, his wife. Long brown hair, unmarked by the gray of age, was caught back at the nape of her neck, and the side of her face that hadn't been caved in was fresh and unlined. Beautiful. And filled with the horror of what had come for her and her son. My gaze went to the child in her arms, his face pressed to her breast and her hand locked around the gaping space at the back of his head that had once been his skull.

"Oh, Keven," I whispered.

It was the boy's name, I knew, taken by the gargoyle that had killed him in her pursuit of Merlin-Morok. The gargoyle that Morgana had become but hadn't been able to stop. I thought back to that day in the garden, when I'd still been new to my Crone status. I'd stood among the strawberries, the sun shining down on my shoulders, and Keven had told me the story of how the battle of Camlann had never been about King Arthur but about the war between Merlin and Morgana. How Merlin had invited Morok into him and turned some of Arthur's soldiers into wolves that he set on Morgana. How she had allowed the Morrigan into her and the Morrigan had turned other soldiers into gargoyles tasked with stopping the wizard.

How there hadn't been room for both witch and goddess in Morgana's body, and so the Morrigan had placed her in one of the gargoyles for safekeeping. How Morgana had been the one to find Merlin-Morok.

"I found him," the gargoyle had told me that day. *"The wizard."* Her words had been few and unflinching, underlined by a grief that had remained raw for fifteen centuries. *"But the mutt's—Lucan's—family stood between us. His wife and son. I didn't even hesitate."*

I looked again at the crushed skulls. I was sure that mother and son had died instantly, but not here. The lack of blood on the floor said that Morok had brought them from somewhere else. That his cruelty had been premeditated. Deliberate.

I was equally sure that if—no, *when*—Lucan returned to himself, he didn't need to see them like this. Or like *that*.

My gaze lingered on the woman's other hand, the one clutched around the boy's back. Three of the fingers were missing, bloodied stumps all that remained where they'd been chewed off. That Lucan had stayed in control of his wolf as long as he had was a miracle, but he wouldn't see it that way. Not if he knew.

And so, while the wolf ate his goat dinner, I gathered sheets from the beds in other huts, rolled the woman and her child onto them, and draped them with the cape and sweater I took from the hooks by the door . Then, while he paced and snarled and threw himself against the chain that held him, I dragged the bodies of his wife and child out through the bailey gates and into the woods where I buried them together beneath a cairn of rocks.

BY THE TIME I RETURNED TO THE HUT, TIRED AND DIRTY BUT satisfied with my work, Lucan was lying quietly, washing his front paws. He looked up at my entrance, but for the first time, he didn't snarl or lunge at me. I saw with surprise that Gus and Harry had moved in, too, claiming the foot of the bed where Gus bathed the little dragon's fuzzy head while Harry rumbled with contentment. The two of them had fended for themselves since our arrival, apparently with considerable success, given the growth spurt Harry appeared to be going through.

I set down the bucket I'd brought back with me. I'd managed—with more effort than I'd expected I would need—to conjure water from the woods. I'd searched high and low for a source inside the bailey on the first day, but the two wells and every bucket I'd found had all been dry, as had the ditch outside the wall. After our first sleep, despite the risk that Morok would sense my presence, I'd tried to pull water from the element, but there had been none. Not a drop. Today, while I'd been putting the last rocks in place over Lucan's wife and son, it had occurred to me that I might have more success among the trees, where things had once grown.

I'd been right, but it had come at a sobering cost. By the time I'd accumulated half a bucket, a dozen trees around me had turned to dust and crumbled out of existence, and I was exhausted. On the bright side, the magick didn't seem to have attracted Morok, and even the goliath's screams had moved away from me while I'd been out there. Whatever the creature wanted, it seemingly wasn't my immediate demise.

On the dark side, given the repercussions, we were going to have to be very careful with this particular resource.

I took a tin cup and a bowl from the table and used the cup to fill the bowl first, then filled the cup itself. I set the bowl on the floor near the end of the bed for Gus and Harry, who both immediately went to it. The cup, I left on the table, and the remaining bucket I held in my hand as I surveyed Lucan.

"If I'm going to give you this, you can't come at me," I said. "Deal?"

The wolf gave no indication of understanding my words, but neither did he move. Gingerly, holding the amber gaze the entire time and hoping he wouldn't take my eye contact as a challenge the way canines did, I walked close enough to set the bucket within his reach, then backed away again. Lucan stood and went to the bucket, and for a few moments, the sounds of lapping—his, Gus's, and Harry's—filled the room. I closed my eyes in a rare moment of appreciation for my own accomplishment.

Goddess, but it felt good to get something right for a—

A familiar, guttural roar split the peace, and my eyes snapped open.

The goliath was back at the gates.

CHAPTER 33

THE GOLIATH.

That fucking goliath.

I balled my shaking hands into fists and paced the floor in front of the door. The creature hadn't come inside the bailey —yet—but every hair on the back of my neck stood on end and my entire body was taut with waiting. With foreboding. I'd heard it in the distance over the last couple of days, but never this close. Never right outside like that.

Had I been wrong? Had the magick I'd used in the woods attracted Morok after all, and the goliath was his way of letting me know he was coming? He'd like that. Making me sweat. Making me wonder. Making me worry because—

Because, fucking hell, I wasn't ready.

"You should have been looking for Morgana's magick," my inner voice whispered. *"The needs of the many, Claire, remember? Looking after Lucan first—"*

Looking after Lucan first was foolish, I snarled at it. *It was stupid and selfish, and I'd do it all over again if I had to, so piss off.*

But I wrapped my arms around myself as guilt settled into my gut. I stared out the open door. I'd stayed with Lucan because I hadn't been able to make myself leave, but had I tried hard enough? Had it really been a case of not being able to go, or just one of wanting—desperately—to stay? I hugged harder. No. I couldn't do this to myself. It was what it was, and beating myself up would only paralyze me. Better to decide what to do now—and to be sure that my choice counted for something. That my efforts to save my protector counted for something. That they hadn't been wasted.

I whirled to face the wolf, and a small start of surprise rippled through me when I saw him sitting tall beside the bucket of water, his demeanor calm as he watched me. Calm and intelligent and …

"You're back," I whispered. "Oh, thank the goddess, you're back."

Elation surged through me. I'd done it. I'd reached Lucan inside his wolf, and now I didn't have to face Morok alone and—

I would have thrown my arms around the shifter right then and there, but Gus leapt down from the bed as I stepped forward, putting himself between us. The cat's back arched high and he hissed at Lucan, and I belatedly remembered caution—and all the reasons for it. I eyed the wolf warily. Was he really back, or …?

The tip of Lucan's tail moved in a single wag. I picked up Gus and set him on the bed beside Harry, who tried to burrow beneath him for protection. "It's okay," I assured the cat. "I'll go slow."

Seeming not to believe me, the cat retreated to the far side of the bed and continued growling. Harry chirped anxiously, followed him, and burrowed afresh.

I turned back to Lucan and held my hands out, palms up.

"First things first," I said. "We need to get the collar off you. May I …?"

The wolf stood up and I inhaled sharply, jerking my hands away. A pained expression crossed his gaze. I gathered my nerve again. I'd appreciated Gus's reminder to be cautious, but I couldn't let it interfere. We needed Lucan back with us. *I* needed him back.

"Sorry," I said to the wolf. "It's been a long few days."

My second attempt to reach for him went better. He stood still, my courage held up, and the collar beneath my fingers was—oh, hell. What even *was* that? I slid my fingers under the collar—or at least tried to—but there was no "under."

It was fused. The freaking thing was fused to its captive.

"Jesus fucking *Christ*," I growled, snatching my hands back and curling them into fists. I stared at my friend, too stunned to feel anything but horror. What in the *hell* was I supposed to do now?

Lucan whined in the back of his throat, clearly asking for an explanation. I hesitated, but there was no good or easy way to tell him, so I blurted it out.

"He fused the collar to you, my friend. I can't take it off."

His cold, wet nose nudged into my hand. I shook my head.

"You don't understand. If I try to remove it, I might ... I might ... "

Another nudge. He knew what I was trying to say, and his response was clear. It was also impossible. I shook my head again, my throat going tight. "I can't," I whispered. "Lucan, I can't. Please don't ask me."

His nose shoved again, cold against my skin. He wasn't just asking, he was insisting. I backed away. Not because I didn't understand. I did. If circumstances were reversed, I would want the same, regardless of the consequences, and he would give it to me. Because his alternative, remaining here the way I'd found him, trapped for eternity, didn't bear thinking about.

But dear goddess, neither did the possibility that I might—

At the gates of the bailey, the goliath screamed again.

"Jesus fucking *hell*," I snarled at it. And then, before I could rethink or reconsider or revert to the coward I wanted to be, I reached for Lucan's collar.

MOROK'S MAGICK FOUGHT MY EVERY EFFORT TO REMOVE IT. Bitterly, furiously. Sweat rolled down my forehead and into my eyes, making them burn, and Lucan writhed beneath my hands, his whimpers reaching into me and slicing open my heart. Time and again, I wanted to give up, to tell him that it was too much—but that would have been the coward's way out.

No matter how hard this was for me, it was a thousand times worse for him, and still he didn't pull away. And as long as he could stay the course, so would I. For what seemed the hundredth time, I re-centered my thoughts and pulled my focus inward. I could feel the magick Morok had placed in the collar. Feel its darkness, its malevolence, its binding—but to what? I squeezed my eyes shut and shook my head in irritation. I was missing something. I had to be missing something.

I sifted through the sensations below my hands and zeroed in on one of the strands tying the collar to Lucan. I followed it into the wolf. Through his fur, his skin, the muscles and vessels and bones, into his very soul itself—and then I understood.

My eyes flew open. Dear goddess, that was it. I released my hold on the collar and cradled the wolf's head in my hands, my fingers cupped around his jaw below his ears. "Lucan," I said, my voice hoarse with fatigue and sorrow, "it's you. You're holding onto the collar."

Amber eyes, clouded by pain, gazed back at me. He didn't understand. I fumbled for the words to explain what I'd found, what I'd felt.

"The magick is dark," I said, "and it's binding itself to another darkness. To things inside you. Calling to them, do you understand?"

No response. I tried again.

"We've all done things we regret. Or not done things. We all have our demons. Morok's magick has attached to yours. Your guilt, your rage …" No understanding flickered in the eyes locked on mine. I tightened my grip on him and growled, "Damn it, Lucan, you weren't responsible for your wife and son dying!"

Fury sparked in his expression, and I felt a rumble beneath the fingers cradled under his throat, but I didn't back down. I couldn't, because now I knew that to do so would be to let

Morok win. To let him have this beautiful, strong, broken soul who deserved so much better—even if it meant his death.

"Listen to me," I insisted. "Listen." The rumble subsided, and I took a deep breath. "I can help pull the magick away," I continued, "but you have to let it go first. You have to *choose* to let it go, Lucan. You have to choose to live—without them, without the guilt, without the blame. It happened. It's done. It can't be changed. But you *can* be."

Then, my gaze not leaving his, I released my hold on his head and reached again for the collar. I gripped it, slid my fingers as far around it as I could, and rested my forehead against my wolf-shifter's.

"Now," I whispered, pouring all the power that had once belonged to a goddess into freeing the friend, the wolf, the man I loved. "Now, Lucan."

The wolf inside the collar thrashed so wildly that it took everything I possessed—physically, mentally, emotionally—to retain my hold on him. He screamed with an agony that scraped my soul raw. Howled with a grief that shredded my heart into tatters. And then he tore free of me.

For a heartbeat, I thought I'd lost him. Time stood utterly still in the face of despair—and then I stared at the collar I still held. It was empty. The wolf it had held was wolf no more.

But looking at the man curled in a fetal position on the packed earth floor, I knew with a sinking heart that the human he'd shifted into was far from whole.

CHAPTER 34

I HAD NO STRENGTH LEFT TO GET LUCAN UP ONTO THE BED, SO I made a bed of sorts on the floor. I staggered from hut to hut, gathering more rough-woven sheets and all of the woolen blankets I could find, uncaring that they were stained with the sweat and fluids of others. I needed to keep the shifter warm, to make him as comfortable as I could so that he could heal.

If he could heal.

I pushed the traitorous thought from my mind as I spread a fourth blanket over the inert form. *He is strong,* I reminded myself. *He'll recover.*

He was *strong,* my doubts whispered back. *Before ...*

I clutched a corner of a blanket in my fist and stared down at the man beneath it. At the gaunt cheeks, their bones too prominent; the matted hair and beard; the closed, sunken eyes, bruised by fatigue.

He'll recover, I told myself again. *He has to.*

And then I crawled under the blankets with him, held his fragility as close as I dared, and with Gus and Harry curled up on the bed above me, fell into an exhausted sleep to the sound of the goliath's screams outside the gate.

THE SHIFTER WAS STILL UNCONSCIOUS WHEN I WOKE. I SPENT the next few hours either sitting in one of the chairs watching for signs of life in the shifter or sleeping fitfully at his side. All while trying not to go utterly mad in this world into which I'd fallen. This splinter. This hell.

At one point, Gus hauled in a small, cloth-wrapped packet of salted meat that he dropped at my feet, smacking away poor Harry when the dragon tried to take some of it. I gave the little dragon an apologetic pat on the head, but I didn't share. He might be hungry, but I knew that he and Gus had plenty to eat in the stables and kitchen. I, on the other hand, had neither the strength nor the will to go in search of anything.

I ate a little of the meat and tucked the rest away for Lucan when he woke, then crept under the blankets again.

I tried not to think too much about Morok and what I would do when I faced him again.

Tried harder not to think about why he hadn't yet appeared. The reasons could be many, I assured myself. It didn't necessarily mean that he'd already found Morgana's magick, or that he'd been able to get past the protection the Morrigan had placed around it. It didn't mean he'd already created the portal back to Earth while I'd looked after Lucan first.

But the very possibility that those things might be true twisted endlessly in my mind, along with the chance that it might all have been for nothing—a chance that grew with every minute Lucan remained unconscious.

That, I tried hardest of all not to think about.

I attempted magick, of course. As soon as I felt I had the capacity, I stripped myself down to bare skin the way the Morrigan had told me to do the last time I'd healed him. I held him close and gathered my magick, my Fire, and reached into him for his—but there had been nothing there. A faint warmth, perhaps, and a heartbeat, but none of the Lucan I had encountered in my healing before. None of the Lucan that I remembered. Only a shell.

I told myself that he was still there, that he was just buried too deeply for me to reach. That he would find his way back if I was patient.

But he and I were both running out of time.

I dressed again and, with a blanket draped over my shoulders in lieu of my battlefield-soiled cloak, sat at the table to nibble a bit more of the salted meat. I needed to keep up my own reserves, and I could go in search of more if—*when*—Lucan woke up.

Over on the bed, Gus stood up, yawned and stretched, and then leapt lightly to the floor. He detoured widely around the sleeping Lucan, pausing to hiss at the prone figure before coming to rub against my leg and receive a pet before continuing out the door.

Harry followed, tripping over his own feet and sneezing on the doorframe as he passed. Flames flared, but I made no move to get up and snuff them out, knowing they would sputter into nothing on their own. The incompleteness of everything in Camlann meant that there wasn't enough substance to sustain a fire. It was both a blessing and a curse. On the one hand, it meant that the bailey, constructed entirely of highly flammable materials, was safe from the dragon.

On the other hand, it rendered useless the few precious herbs I still carried, because without fire, I couldn't heat the water needed to steep them.

I'd tried magick there, too, but I'd been so drained after removing Lucan's collar that I'd misjudged and succeeded only in evaporating the precious little water that remained from the woods. I might be able to manage now, but I would have to go back to the woods first, and—

The goliath screamed at the gate.

I clenched my jaw. If worrying over Lucan didn't drive me mad, that would.

I wrapped the blanket tighter and held it in place with crossed arms as I stood and went to the door that I never bothered closing. Leaving it open meant Gus and Harry could come and go as they pleased, and with no one else here—no one alive, anyway, I thought as my gaze tracked (as it always did) the scattered bodies—there was no need of privacy or worry for our security. The goliath screamed again.

Well. Maybe there *were* great worries for our security, but let's face it, if the goliath decided to come through the gate and into the bailey, a door wouldn't even slow it down.

I turned my gaze up the hill toward another wooden wall and the top of the tower jutting above it. The keep, or castle, where King Arthur himself would have lived. Surprisingly, it looked to be built of stone, which would have put him centuries ahead of castle-building in general, and part of me itched to explore the structure. To know that King Arthur had been real, to stand in the space where he had lived and slept, eaten and governed—once, the dewy-eyed teenager in me would have swooned at the idea.

Once, before I'd learned the truth about the fabled king and his castle. Not to mention before I'd crossed the battlefield of Camlann and seen firsthand the glories of medieval war.

My mouth twisted, and the tiny thrill that had run through me dissipated the way Harry's flames on the doorframe had.

Life had been much simpler as a dewy-eyed teenager, I thought, with no small amount of nostalgia. Hell, life had been much simpler as a dewy-eyed grandmother before finding myself catapulted into this magickal mayhem.

Movement out in the yard between huts caught my eye, and I watched Gus trotting back in my direction. Head and tail held high, he carried what looked like a bird, and the ever-present Harry pranced behind him with the remains of a rat clamped in his jaws—identifiable by the long tail trailing from it.

The little dragon had grown again, I realized with a start. He was easily twice Gus's size, wing-nubs had become actual wings (albeit, still tiny ones), and while feathers still covered his body, they'd begun to give way to scales on his head, giving him a patchwork—and rather homely—appearance.

A face only a mother could love, I thought with a smile as Gus looked back to make sure his charge was following.

The goliath screamed again as the animals paraded past me into the hut, and I lifted my gaze from them to glare in the direction of the bailey gates. What in the name of the goddess did it want? Me? Gus again? Why didn't it just come in after us? The screeching was driving me insane. It never came closer than the gates, never came inside the bailey. It was as bad as the damned crows had been back at the Earth house. It just hung around and made noise, as if it was taunting me, or—

Every part of my being went still. My breath, my mind, my center.

Or.

Or it was trying to get my attention.

Like the damned crows had done.

The idea was ludicrous. At the same time, it wasn't. My mind skipped across a dozen thoughts like a flat stone across the surface of a pond. The pain I'd heard in its cries—first in my own world and now here. The way it hadn't killed Gus. The way it *had* listened to me and responded. The way its screams had moved away from me when I'd gone to the woods to bury Lucan's wife and son and to pull water from the trees, as if ...

As if it wanted me to follow. As if it was trying to lead me somewhere.

No. I shook my head. Because even if I was right, even if it was trying to get my attention, what if it was a trap? What if it led me to Morok? What if—

The goliath screamed once more. This time, I let my eyes drift shut and I listened. I listened to the sound rolling through the bailey and to the pain underlying it. I listened, I heard, and I breathed. A soft, small stillness formed in my core, and within it, a possibility.

"Because what if," I murmured under my breath, "it's something else?"

A hand settled on my shoulder, and I nearly jumped out of my skin.

CHAPTER 35

GOLIATH FORGOTTEN, MY BLANKET DROPPED TO THE FLOOR AS I swung around so fast that I almost fell against the man who had at last risen from the floor and come to join me. I stared into the familiar amber eyes, not quite trusting my own.

"You're awake?" I whispered. I let my gaze travel his length, absorbing every detail, every nuance. He'd tied back his long hair and found clothes somewhere. I hadn't even heard him moving around, but he'd already dressed in a loose, unbleached shirt and a pair of brown trousers cinched at the waist with a cord. They did nothing to hide his thinness, but I didn't care. It mattered only that he'd survived Morok's magick—and mine—and dear goddess, it was good to see him.

"You're awake," I repeated without the question mark. "I didn't—"

"Kill me?" The corner of Lucan's mouth quirked, but the smile didn't quite reach his amber eyes. "No, but I have to admit that it felt like you might."

Remembered despair crushed my heart and the grief I'd narrowly avoided gripped my throat. I inhaled a ragged breath and took an involuntary step back.

"Don't," I said. "Don't even joke about it. I was—" I broke off as he swayed on his feet. Shoving my angst into a mental closet to deal with another time, I took Lucan's arm. "You're exhausted. Come and sit."

Shaking his head, he resisted my attempt to steer him toward the table. "We don't have time. Morok—"

The goliath's scream cut him off. His head snapped around toward the door., and for the breadth of a heartbeat, his form blurred. Then it solidified again, and he staggered, falling against me. I grunted under his weight. He might be thin, but he was still a substantial man.

Shock flickered across his white face, mirroring my own.

"I can't—" he began hoarsely.

"Of course not," I said, with all the reassurance I could muster. All the reassurance I didn't feel, because never had I—

I pushed the thought away, unable to finish it—not daring to let myself—and turned to practicalities. Specifically, the fear that I couldn't hold him up much longer. I injected a brisk note into my voice. "It's no wonder, after what you've been through. You need more rest, that's all."

I half led, half carried him back toward the bed—the real one this time, not the one on the floor. Gus was still there with his prize, but Harry had retreated under the bed with only the tip of his blue tail poking out.

The cat arched and growled at our approach, and when I tried to shoo him away, he retreated into the back corner, hissing at the shifter as Lucan sagged onto the edge of the bed. I tossed the remains of the cat's bird onto the floor, hoping he'd follow, but his growls only grew higher in pitch, punctuated by spitting.

"Damned cat never did like me," Lucan muttered. "Must be the wolf."

"Must be." I said, trying not to puff between words. I rested my hands on my thighs and willed my heartbeat to slow after the exertions of getting him across the room. I'd deal with Gus when I could breathe again.

"Are you okay?"

"I'm fine," I said. "Just not as young as I used to be." No longer on the verge of collapse myself, I reached past him to pull Gus across the bed and into my arms to soothe him. Gus, however, was having none of it. The cat promptly sank every one of his claws into my skin, launched himself from my shoulder, and belted out of the hut as if all the hounds of hell were after him.

I yelped as much in surprise as in pain, then danced out of the way as the blue patchwork fluff-ball that was Harry bolted out from under the bed and screeched after him—literally—only to turn at the door, run back, seize the discarded bird remains, and run out again.

"What," Lucan asked slowly, "was *that?*"

"A long story," I replied with a sigh as I rubbed my fiery puncture wounds. My many puncture wounds. Damned cat. "His name is—"

Another scream from the goliath cut me off. I watched Lucan, but apart from a slight tightening around his mouth, there was no reaction. No attempt to morph into wolf-form. The thought I hadn't finished before surfaced again. This time, I let it complete itself in all its impossibility, all its enormity.

Never had I seen one of the protectors unable to shift into his wolf, regardless of injuries. Even Bedivere ... after Cernunnos ... even then.

Grimly, I held back a shudder at the memory, then I pressed my lips together against the deep, deep misgiving that settled over me. This was so not good. And so not the kind of thing that was likely to be made better by a nap. I needed to think. Needed to rethink. Needed to—

Lucan's hand closed over mine and pressed gently. I stared down at I, and then at the bowed head of the man it belonged to. My not-protector, my shifter ... my broken, broken friend. The damage done to him by Morok was so much more than I'd been able to undo in two short days. Perhaps if we had more time ... but we didn't.

We'd run out of that particular commodity. Me. Lucan. The world.

I knew what I had to do.

And I'd be doing it alone.

ALONE.

I'd come all this way and, against all odds, I'd actually found Lucan, and I was still going to have to face Morok alone.

I stared down at the sleeping man in the bed. His breathing was shallow, his eyes closed, and tawny lashes rested against cheeks made dark by the grime I hadn't had water enough to wash from his skin. It hadn't taken him long to drift off. I'd been glad when he did, in part because he'd needed the sleep, but mostly because I hadn't wanted to argue with him about what I was going to do.

Perversely, I now wished he would wake up so that I could say goodbye … just in case.

But he stayed asleep, even when I pulled the rough blankets up over his shoulders and tucked them under his chin. Leaning down, I pressed my lips to his forehead, lingering for a moment as I committed his warmth to memory … again, just in case.

I wished I'd had time to wash him. I wished he could come with me. I wished I could leave him knowing that he would be safe without me, that he would survive and find a way back to our own world. I wished that he could be whole again. And happy. I wished more than anything that he could be happy. Goddess knew he deserved it.

And then I straightened and turned toward the door, because I could control none of that. Influence none of it. Expect none of it. His future and mine were too entangled in the vagaries of the gods. What was, was, and what would be, would be, regardless of what we wished for. Before I'd even entered the Otherworld, I'd known that. Known that, even if by some miracle I found him, neither of us was likely to survive what came next.

Morok had come *so* close to defeating me in New York that day that I still woke sometimes with the taste of concrete dust in my mouth. Still saw the building crumbling around me and the Crones hanging almost lifeless in the air. Still heard his invective-filled *"bitch"* ringing in my ears as he unleashed his magick on me.

I'd almost died that day, and that had been with Lucan and the other shifters there to back me up. Here, Morok had the powers taken from him when the Morrigan split Camlann from the rest of the world, plus the ones he'd retained when I'd faced him in that tower. And I had—

I stopped in the doorway and scanned the room, but there was nothing. My cloak, beyond the repair of the magick Baba Yaga had restored to it, remained balled up in the rucksack, and I no longer had my staff. That left—

A small head butted up against my shin, and I looked down at the cat pressing against my ankle while his ever-present dragon shadow chased his tail. My throat tightened and tears burned behind my eyes. Gus. It left Gus.

I leaned down and rubbed my hand over the length of my beloved companion from head to tail, imprinting the feel of his fur and the arch of his back on my hand, my heart. We'd been through so very much together, he and I, I thought wistfully. I wanted—fiercely and desperately—to take him with me, but I couldn't risk the distraction. If I was wrong about what the goliath wanted and Morok was at the end of this little foray after all, I would need every ounce of focus I possessed. I wouldn't get a second chance.

I gave Gus a final rub, patted Harry's patchwork head, and smiled down through my tears at the odd pair.

"Be good," I told them, "and watch out for one another."

I shooed Gus into the hut, Harry predictably followed, and I shut everyone I loved inside, where they stood a chance of remaining safe. Of living a little while longer than I might.

The goliath screamed again.

CHAPTER 36

THE GOLIATH WAS NOWHERE TO BE SEEN WHEN I STEPPED through the gates and onto the road leading into the woods. I stood for several minutes, listening to the silence, straining to hear something—anything—but, as usual in this godforsaken place, not so much as a leaf stirred on a branch. If I ever made it back to my own world, I would never again take sound for granted, I thought. The wind, birds, voices other than the ones in my head ... goddess, but I longed to hear them all again. Longed to hear—

A familiar scream came from the woods to my left, and I stared into the trees. I supposed I could have thought deep thoughts or made a momentous decision of some kind, but I didn't. I just stared and sighed, and then I stepped off the road and into the woods, pushing through the underbrush in the direction of the sound.

There were no trails, and the going was rough. More than once, as I staggered and recovered from the uneven ground, I thought about turning back from what was surely a fool's errand. More than once, I convinced myself to keep going, because whatever this was going to be, I just wanted it over with.

Most often of all, I wished it already was—no matter the outcome.

My lungs heaved like bellows and my palm itched for the feel of the staff that Lucan had carved for me. I wished I still had it for many reasons: its flair for taking the legs out from under an unsuspecting opponent, its ability to channel and concentrate my magick, its usefulness in clearing a path ...

But, mostly, its comfort.

The forest closed behind me as I forged my way through,

erasing all trace of my passage. It occurred to me that, whether or not I found the goliath, I would be hard pressed to find my way back to the gates. However, it was too late to leave a trail of breadcrumbs—even if I'd had access to bread —and so I continued.

Whenever I stopped to catch my breath or get my bearings, the goliath would scream again, and I would adjust my course accordingly. I had no idea of the passage of time. Frankly, I hadn't had much sense of time since I'd landed in the Otherworld where there had been no day or night. These days—so to speak—I slept when I was tired, pulled water from the trees when I was thirsty, and went in search of something edible when I got hungry.

And, apparently, I walked when the goliath screamed.

Several times, I thought I'd spotted it through the trees and my heart gave a great thud against my ribs, though I wasn't sure whether it was in anticipation or foreboding. Each time, however, it turned out to be a trick of the shadows, or perhaps my imagination, and my steps would resume.

Then, when my hair clung damply to my forehead and neck, and my armpits were drenched with sweat and my legs ached with effort, I staggered out of the woods and almost fell at the foot of a small rise—topped by the goliath I'd been pursuing. I stumbled to a halt, shock robbing me of the little bit of breath remaining after my trek.

For a long moment, the monster and I stared at one another, with it looking down and me looking way, way up. I had forgotten how very tall it was. How huge. How mountainously terrifying. Surreptitiously, just in case, I began to gather my magick, reaching down into the soil for Earth and into my core for Fire, readying myself for battle.

But the goliath didn't attack. Instead, it tipped back its head and wailed, and then it shuffled aside to reveal a boulder that had been at its back. With my heat coiled at the ready in my palms, I looked between boulder and monster.

"You brought me here for that?" I asked. The goliath swayed back and forth on its trunk-like legs. Not quite an affirmative, but not a negative, either. Slowly, my legs protesting every step, I climbed the rise to the boulder's edge. Then, keeping one eye on my companion, I studied the rock. It was unremarkable in every way that I could see. Large and gray as boulders tended to be, its edges softened by millennia of erosion and its surface patchy with lichens, and ...

And then I saw the letters carved into it and the slot cut into its top. A thrill shot through me, and I forgot how to breathe.

"Fuck," I whispered. A huge stone sitting near the battlefield of Camlann, outside the walls of Camelot, with letters carved into it and a slot as if it had once held something. Something that had been pulled from it.

Holy mother of everything that ever was or would be or might be or ...

The goliath shambled over to join me, but I felt no need to retreat. Instead, I watched as it bowed its head and rested a massive hand atop the boulder and then, with a claw on its other hand, traced a line beneath the letters. Letters that formed words I didn't need to read to know: *Whoso pulleth out this sword from this stone, is right wise King born of all England.*

Another thrill went through me, this one tinged with sorrow. Grief.

"Dear goddess," I whispered.

I put an involuntary hand out to cover the goliath's. It flinched beneath my touch but didn't draw back. Pieces of the puzzle dropped into place: the pain underlying the goliath's cries, the apparent mercy it—*he*—had shown toward Gus, and ...

And the way it had pushed me away from the portal in New York, saving me from going through with Lucan and Morok and ...

My fingers closed around the huge granite paw that was

covered in a wolf's fur. *An unfortunate merging of Merlin and Morgana's magick,* Lucan had said. But there was more to it. More as in *someone,* I thought. Someone who had been caught between the wizard he believed in and the sister he loved. A king.

"You're him," I said, my voice cracking. "You're—"

A twig snapped behind us, and I whirled, the Fire I'd banked springing back into my palms as I crouched in readiness, certain that this was it. This was my time. But my gaze fell on a familiar figure, and my knees sagged in relief as I reabsorbed the magick yet again, grateful that I'd at least mastered that much control.

"Lucan," I said. "You scared me half to death. I can't believe you managed to follow me here. I thought—"

But I didn't have a chance to finish what I thought. The goliath stepped between me and the wolf-shifter and screamed so loudly that I slapped my hands over my ears to protect them. I stared in shock at the carved muscles of its—his— back. That hadn't been pain in his voice, it had been challenge. Defiance. Fury.

In the space of a heartbeat, my misgivings returned, magnified by a thousand. I'd been right. It was a trap. Former king or not, the goliath *had* lured me here to face Morok, and now Lucan had followed me, and he wasn't strong enough to fight, and Morok would do to him again what he'd done before. Collar him, imprison him, degrade him beyond endurance.

I could not—would not—let that happen.

I could face Morok. I could face death. But I could not face that.

I darted around the goliath's bulk, aiming a fireball at it as I slammed my intent into the soil beneath me and called again on Earth. "Run!" I yelled at Lucan. "It's a trap!"

Unfazed by the flames burning the sparse hair from its body, the goliath picked me up and set me behind it again. It roared as it held me there, struggling in its hold. Shoving my panic aside along with my fear for Lucan, who would still be weakened by his ordeal, I made myself still. Made myself center. Made myself—

Beyond the goliath, out of my sight, Lucan laughed. My focus wavered. The goliath roared once more, again without pain or grief, again in fury. A slow, awful realization began to unfurl in me, splitting my mind in two. Denial on one side. Horrified insight on the other.

Ice water filled my lungs, and I spun backward through a vortex of time and memories into terror. Into dark. Into a cell where I had heard this laughter once before. A cell where I had faced Morok in the guise of another.

Then, it had been Kate. Now ...

Now, it was not.

Lucan's voice laughed again.

CHAPTER 37

I DON'T KNOW WHERE THE CALM CAME FROM THAT ENVELOPED me. I had no reason to be calm. No right, even. Not when my entire existence had just imploded the way it had. And certainly not when I had made such a monumental error.

How? A part of me wondered. How did I miss it?

But the calm was there nonetheless, and so I laid a gentle hand on the goliath's arm, and when his long-muzzled head swung around to look at me, I said, "It's okay. I know who he is."

I know who he is. The words elicited a grunt from the goliath and nothing from me. No feeling at all. Briefly, I examined the idea. Huh. That must be it. No feeling. No fear, not even anger. Just calm and—

"It was a trap, all right," Lucan's voice said cheerfully. "Thank you for walking into it—and for finding what I was looking for. You've saved me a great deal of trouble."

Lucan's voice, but not Lucan's voice.

I stepped around the goliath and stared at the man climbing the slope to join me. At the gaunt body beneath the coarse clothes, the familiar face behind the beard and grime, the tawny eyes that held not a trace of the man I had known.

Lucan, but not Lucan.

He reached my side, and I tipped my head back. Challenging the calm, daring myself to feel, I made myself look deeper, to the god beneath. The god that had deceived me not once, but twice.

Morok, in Lucan's body.

Lucan, gone.

I waited for the grief, but there was still nothing. Not so much as a twinge. I replayed Lucan's—Morok's—words in my

201

head. What did he mean, I'd found what he was looking for? I glanced at our surroundings: the woods behind Luc—Morok, the rise where we stood, and the grass trampled flat by the goliath's feet. The only thing here was the stone where—

Understanding was swift and blinding, and it hit me like a sucker punch.

Well, shit, I thought, and it was the beginning of the end of my calm. Because, of course. What place was more appropriate for hiding Morgana's magick than the stone that had once held Excalibur itself? The power to make a king—

Or to remake a god.

Slowly, I turned back to face Lucan. Slowly, I raised my gaze to the god who had taken his body. Slowly, the finality hit me. This was it. The final showdown between me and—

The air wheezed from my lungs and all pretense at calm fled.

Jesus fuck. I was going to have to fight the wolf-shifter I'd come to love.

EVERYTHING HAPPENED AT ONCE, SO FAST THAT I GAVE UP trying to keep track.

I saw Morok's intent in Lucan's eyes before he moved. In the same instant, the goliath dived between us and absorbed the full impact of the magick that had been intended to kill me. Then, even as he flew backward under the impact, he swung a mighty arm at the god, knocking him ass over teakettle down the slope. I flinched at the crunch of breaking bone.

As powerful as he was, the god inhabited a corporeal body that—while also immortal—could still be injured, and his howl of pain reverberated over the hill and twisted through my heart.

Lucan, I thought. But I forced myself to turn away from where he lay on the ground.

Not Lucan, I reminded myself as I crawled to the felled goliath's side. Not Lucan at all. Not anymore. Not after what I'd seen done to Kate before him.

My breath caught as I reached the goliath, and I wanted to weep at the damage Morok had inflicted. Half the creature's face was gone, the sparse fur was singed from his body, and his massive, muscular chest torso was cracked almost in two. If Morok's blast had hit me, unprepared as I was ...

I touched the goliath's arm. He turned his head and mournfully regarded me with his one remaining eye. I resisted the urge to look away from the wound. Away from his sadness.

"The stone!" I said urgently. "Does it open? Do you know how?"

Another howl came from Morok, this one of rage. I looked over my shoulder as the god forced Lucan's body to its feet and launched himself up the hill, slowed but not stopped by the shattered, bloody end of the shinbone protruding from his pant leg. He'd hobbled fewer than a half dozen steps when Harry and Gus tumbled out of the woods behind him, Harry half running and half awkwardly, not-quite flying as his little wings beat furiously at the air.

My instinct to protect them was instantaneous and fierce. I pushed it aside. We were fighting for more than our own existence now—all of us—and they were beyond my protection. Me, my cat, the little dragon, the goliath. All were needed to fight Morok if we were going to stop him. And *I* needed my furred and feathered friends to distract him so I could get to Morgana's magick before he did.

A hissing, yowling Gus launched onto Morok-Lucan's shoulders and clung there, eliciting a shriek from the god who hadn't seen him coming. Morok responded in an all-too human way, dancing in a circle as he grabbed at the feline, but Gus's claws were well and truly sunk into Lucan's skin and he wasn't letting go. And Harry wasn't letting him fight the battle alone.

The gutsy little dragon joined the fray and set fire to Lucan's pant leg—on purpose. My heart swelled for an instant with pride in him and gratitude for them both, and then it collapsed under the pain of the sacrifice I knew they were about to make. Gus, Harry, Lucan, the goliath.

I had to make it count. I *would* make it count.

Unable to get to its feet, the goliath pulled itself, hand over hand, across the trampled grass toward the stone. There, it raised itself up on one elbow and brought its other fist down on the stone that had once made it king. Again and again and again, all without effect. A cat screamed behind me. *Gus.*

Morok-Lucan tossed aside a limp bundle as I whirled. Both pain and fury ripped through me, but even as I rooted myself to Earth and raised Fire and called on Air and Water, I knew the futility of raising my power. Without whatever was in that stone, without Morgana's magick, I still had only half the power of the dark god. Half the power and—

The little dragon that had launched himself at Morok-Lucan sailed through the air to land unmoving beside his muzzer, and my heart shattered into a thousand splinters. *Half the power*, the remains of it whispered as it died alongside the only remaining friends that I'd had. *Half the power, and none of the will.*

My connection to the elements faltered. Behind me, the goliath slammed his fist down again, *boom!* And then, *crack!*

The stone had broken.

CHAPTER 38

IT WAS A RACE TO SEE WHO WOULD GET TO IT FIRST. IT HAD always been a race. We'd just neither of us foreseen how it would end.

An orb of white light sat where the stone had cleaved in two beside the unmoving goliath. Morok hobbled past me, shoving me to the ground before I'd taken a single step. His hands closed around the light and lifted it, cradled it, and held it high in triumph as my connection to my magick withered inside me.

He'd won. He'd won, and now he would—

Morok smashed the orb against the stone that had housed it. Once, twice ... the third time, it smashed into shards. A beam of light shot up from it into the sky and exploded in a shower of sparks. My hand involuntarily twitched as if to reach for it—for them—but it was too late. Whatever had been in the orb was gone, taking hope with it.

Morok's included.

Nothing. There had been nothing. The orb had been a decoy. I watched incredulity chase disbelief across the dark god's expression as he stared upward, hands outstretched to receive a gift that was never coming. I chuckled. Then I chortled. Then I laughed. I sat on the grass, legs outstretched before me and arms braced behind me, and I laughed and laughed and laughed. Then, as the rage-filled face of Lucan-no-more turned toward me and all the implications of my situation sank in, laughter strangled into a sob in my throat.

The orb had been a decoy.

We weren't done. Morgana's magick was still out there somewhere, and there was still a chance, and Jesus *fuck*, would this hell never end? I couldn't do this anymore. Not alone. I'd thought I could when I left the others in the hut, but I'd been wrong. I *had* needed them. I'd needed to know that someone waited for my return. Needed to have something to fight for. But now they were all gone—Lucan, Gus, Harry, even the goliath—and it was just me and Morok locked in this fucking game and—

Twenty feet away, Morok gathered his power. It boiled like red-black clouds around him, swallowed him, began to coalesce in his outstretched, clawed hands.

I tried to make myself care. Tried, even, to rouse the doggedness at my core. Neither responded. I slid my fingers into my front pocket and curled my fingers around the Thor figurine. I took a deep breath unscented by my grandson's smell. I exhaled.

Done, I thought. *I am so very, very—*

An angry bellow shattered my giving-up, and my eyes flew open before I could stop them. Morok's angry power clouds had dissipated, and flames engulfed him instead. Clear, pure, violet flames. I stared in incomprehension.

White flashed to the left and my gaze darted to the source. A woman. There was a woman coming along the hillside. A woman with long gray hair lifting back from a pale face and cloaked shoulders as she moved, the skirts of her dress dragging at her feet. The white flash that had drawn my attention was leaving hands that swirled through the air and shooting across the space between her and Morok. It erupted into more violet around him—and I knew in an instant what the Morrigan had done.

Morgana. Jesus fucking Christ on a cracker, the goddess hadn't hidden Morgana's magick at all—she'd left it in the woman's own form.

And now Morok knew, too.

The dark god staggered out of the purple flames and swayed on his feet, then recovered his balance—and his focus. Again, his hands moved in the air. Again, the darkness swirled around him. With a single wave, he parried a fresh burst of violet fire.

Morgana's magick had been enough to slow and distract him, but it would not be enough to stop him. But maybe between the two of us ...

I leapt to my feet with an agility I'd forgotten I possessed— that I'd almost lost beneath the weight of Camlann itself. My right hand closed into a fist over empty air, and for the breath of an instant, I felt the absence of my staff with a keenness that was physical. Visceral. But red fire clashed with violet, and I had no time to mourn either the loss of the staff or that of its creator.

Planting my feet in the grass, I called once more on Earth. The element responded so fast that the shock of its connection rocked me back on my heels. Swiftly, I reached for the Fire at my core, and before Morok could release his own magick, threw all the heat at him that I could muster, grounded in the Earth element itself.

It was enough to have taken out a dozen shades, if those had been its target. But instead, it only served to infuriate the dark god further. He swept an arm in a wide circle and gathered everything I'd just sent at him, wrapped it into his own and—

A small ball of blue fury slammed into the side of Morok's head, darted away, and returned to strike again. The churning black-red clouds surrounding the god thinned and scattered. He flapped an arm at the attacking dragon, but Harry dodged his blows and dropped on his next pass to slam into the bone that protruded from Lucan's leg. The dark god bellowed, stumbled, and fell to the ground beside the fallen goliath. A stone hand stirred and stretched. Claws closed over the broken shinbone. The goliath squeezed.

The god's screech was altogether human in its agony— and altogether Lucan's. The sound pierced my core itself and, for an instant, I forgot that god and shifter were one. Forgot that I had already lost my protector, my friend. I stepped toward him, wanting—needing—to ease his pain.

A form stepped in front of me, and I brought myself up short. Morgana. I'd forgotten her, too, for a moment, but now I remembered. I remembered who she was—and who Morok wasn't.

Morgana held her hands out to me, and I stared down at them and then at her—the first of us. The original Crone, who had given herself up to the goddess she had served so that Morok might be stopped. Her brown eyes held no expression, but the lines of her face held the memories of a lifetime. Memories of wisdom and sacrifice and love. Memories of the woman she had been and the gargoyle she had become. Memories of the goddess herself.

And memories of the magick I needed.

I extended my hands to meet hers. "I'm ready," I said.

But I wasn't. Not for this.

Morgana's fingers clamped onto mine like a vise. Her spine arched, her head dropped back on her shoulders, and her cloak fell to the ground as she opened her mouth in a shriek that rivaled any I'd ever heard. A shriek that carried power, portent, pain—and fifteen centuries of betrayal. It rolled across the hill and into the forest, made Morok slap his hands over Lucan's ears, sent Harry scurrying for the comfort of his fallen friend's body, and shook the foundation of Camlann itself. And then it rolled back again to slam into me in a wave of sound and power.

Not magick. Power.

Oh, magick was in there, too, but this ... this was more. This was power that rose to meet a counterpart that already existed in me. Power that was familiar. Power that I didn't just recognize but *knew*.

And it belonged not to Morgana, but to the Morrigan herself.

I pulled my hands away, but it was too late. The shell that

was Morgana collapsed at my feet, its purpose fulfilled, drained of that which ricocheted through every cell of my being, tearing me open and stitching me together again in the same instant, the same breath—but not the same existence. Already saturated with what it had absorbed from the Morrigan's pendant that day in New York, my very human body did. everything it could to reject this new burden, but to no avail.

Half the power of a goddess—a true half this time, not half of half of what had been left over from dozens of splinters—settled in as if it owned me and made me every inch as powerful as the god I fought.

And then it joined with Morgana's magick.

CHAPTER 39

A NEW SHRIEK HIT MY EARS AND I RAISED MY GAZE FROM Morgana's shell in time to see Morok slam the goliath's body into the ground with a blast of crimson.

Arthur, my inner voice reminded me. *His name was Arthur.*

"You *witch*!" Morok screamed, incandescent with rage as he limped across the grass and thrust his face into mine. "You utter, absolute, fucking *witch*! I will tear you limb from limb, do you hear me? That magick is *mine.*"

His words hit me like slaps to the face. His spittle, like an undesired shower. Part of me wanted to draw back in distaste, but part of me wanted to stare into him—all the way into his soul—because this, all of this, had an eerie familiarity about it that made me shiver. Made me cringe. Made me angrier with every second I thought about it.

What had happened between him and the Morrigan had been more than just a lover's spat. It had been me and Jeff all over again. A spoiled, insecure excuse for a male who needed to boost his own ego through cheating and controlling and— freaking hell, Freya hadn't been kidding about the gods being just as petty as the humans who created them, had she?

I lifted my chin and met the amber eyes stare for stare. Met them, wept inside for the man who had once looked at me through them, and vowed, once and for all, to finish the god who had taken them. Who had taken so much from so many.

A flicker of wariness crossed the gaze holding mine, and then something deeper, more cunning. I felt the blow coming. I didn't wait for it to land. I stepped to the right and ducked, pulled together the power that sat ready in me, and threw it at Morok. He stumbled and fell to Lucan's knees. He struggled to rise and fell forward onto his hands. His power surged and fizzled, waxed and waned. Puzzled disbelief clouded his eyes.

"You can't," he said. "You're not enough."

But I was. I was more than enough. And so was the Morrigan. And so had Morgana been. And together? Together, we were fucking brilliant.

My hands flashed through the air, drawing sigils from another's memory, tying magick and power together. I would leave no room for error. *Could* leave no room for error. I'd seen what using my magick did to this world when I pulled water from the trees in the woods. I would have one chance to do this, and one chance only.

"Stop," Morok said. He tried to rise again, and I paused to loop an invisible cord of Earth around his wrists and another around his ankles.

"It doesn't have to end like this," he said. "We can talk. Come to an agreement."

I considered binding his mouth, too, but a vindictive side of me—or perhaps it belonged to the Morrigan—rather liked hearing him beg. I went back to assembling my magick.

"You don't want to do this," he growled. "Think of the repercussions. Think of what you'll be destroying."

I smiled grimly.

"Claire," he said hoarsely. Only this time, it wasn't him. It wasn't Morok.

My hands stilled in mid-air. Slowly, I took my gaze from them to meet the amber one again. The amber one with Lucan behind it. The real Lucan. Air left my lungs as if from a deflating balloon, and my intent faltered.

He was still in there. Jesus *fuck*, Lucan was still in there, and Morok had let him through. Had let me see him.

I let my hands drift back to my sides as Lucan's expression softened and, for a heartbeat, a moment suspended in time itself, the connection between us was there again. Whole. Ours. Gratitude and love swelled in me, ached through me, and then faded in the face of the determination hardening the eyes I loved so much.

"Now," Lucan said. "Do it *now.*"

But even as the words formed on his lips, Morok was back and pushing to his feet, because my hesitation had been just enough to loosen his bonds, and then he was standing, and he was laughing and—

I faltered, and then fury twisted through me. Became me. Was me. I hadn't finished weaving all that I wanted, but it would be enough. Just like me and the Morrigan.

I raised my hands to the sigils that hung, glowing, in the air between me and the dark god. Swiftly, before Morok could stop me, I swept the seething energy into a haphazard ball and let fly, holding back nothing.

"You are enough," I whispered to it.

The ball of sigils and intention lifted Morok from his feet and encased him in a sphere a half dozen feet above the ground. It hung without moving for an instant as his arms beat against its walls, and then it began to shrink. The god within shrieked with impotent rage as the walls closed, feeling the imminence of his own death pressing in on him. His very extinction. His—

"*Claire,*" Lucan's hoarse voice said in my memory.

Fuck.

My hands released the magick and fell back to my sides as ice washed through me. I couldn't do it. Not knowing that Lucan was still in there somewhere. If I killed him, Morok would win. I couldn't give up like that. There had to be another way. I would *make* another way.

I reached to pull back on the magick, but it fought my hold and demanded release. Demanded its sacrifice, its— blood? I quailed inside at the realization, and my grip on the power slipped. Oh shit. Blood magick. I'd tapped into blood magick, and it wouldn't stop until it had consumed what I had created it to consume. Unless—

I sketched a new sigil in the air and threw it at the sphere holding the human figure that was both Morok and Lucan. It bucked under the impact and then, like a living cell, began to divide—along with the man inside it. Morok's screams turned from fury to terror, and then to agony, and then doubled as his figure separated—no, tore—into two. One Lucan, and one ... not.

One voice ended abruptly as Lucan tumbled from his half of the sphere to lie crumpled on the grass below. The other continued. Swiftly, I threw my intent into the sphere holding Morok to ensure he didn't follow Lucan to the ground.

And then Camlann began to crumble into dust.

I HEARD THE FALLING-APART BEFORE I SAW IT. IT WAS LIKE A faint underscore to the dark god's agony, like a whisper carried on a breeze, except there was no breeze. On the far edge of the woods through which I'd followed the goliath, the trees began to fall away. Not fall, but fall away, as if into a great chasm slowly expanding toward us. Panic gripped me for a moment as I watched the forest disappear one row at a time, but it didn't last because there was no point to it. Not anymore.

I had done all that I could. *Been* all that I could.

I had stopped Morok and saved what remained of my world. My grandson would grow up and perhaps have grandchildren of his own one day. Keven and the house would have one another for as long as they lasted. And I—I would die with the man whose life I had come to save.

All in all, it wasn't a bad end.

Morok's screams had stopped. The sphere that contained him was the size of a beach ball now. If he still lived within it, he gave no sign. It was almost anticlimactic, I thought.

Except, perhaps, for that part. I looked down at my feet as the ground trembled. The Between was getting closer.

That's what the chasm was. The Between, doing what it did. Devouring the splinter, unmaking what had once been made. It wouldn't be long, now.

I eased myself down beside Lucan. With gentle fingers, I brushed the hair back from his face, studying the familiar lines and planes and wishing again that I had taken the time to wash the dirt from his skin. Though I supposed the Between wouldn't care.

I cradled one of his hands in both of mine as I watched another row of trees fall. My gaze traveled over the tower of Camelot, still visible above the trees, then to the battlefield we had crossed when we first came through the door from the Otherworld, then settled on the tinier battleground that the hill had become. I blinked back tears as I took in the crumpled form of Morgana. Swallowed the ache in my throat as I looked at the unmoving goliath who had once been king.

Caught back a sob as my gaze settled on the still body of Gus and the little blue dragon that flapped in ragged circles above him, calling for his muzzer. What little remained of my heart quietly shattered.

Jesus fuck, Harry.

Tears streaming, I swiped the back of one hand under my nose. Dear goddess, as much as I had known that it would end like this, I wished it could have been different. Wished with all my soul that there could have been less death and more life. More hope. If not for me, then at least for the ones who had loved me and followed me and fought for me. They had deserved so much more than this. So much better.

The dragon's flight smoothed out as he mastered his wings. I watched through my tears as he flapped faster, and a small whirlwind formed over Gus in his wake. Bits of dead grass and dust swirled in circles, drifting over the ginger fur. Harry's path widened and then, abruptly, he changed direction and flew toward the broken stone at the top of the hill. The vortex he'd created around Gus followed, and dragon and whirlwind both centered over the stone. Harry's speed increased again, and the vortex picked up more debris, drawing in whatever it could reach and lifting the hair from my shoulders—probably the first wind to touch Camlann since the split. Or at least since the portal had brought Morok and Lucan and the goliath here from Earth, because that had likely come with a vortex, too. Just like the one that had formed in New—

I gave a wheeze and stared at the widening swirl. A vortex had formed in New York, too, fed by Morok spinning at its center. It had been the precursor to the portal, what had powered it—or, rather, what had drawn in the power Morok needed from the Crones.

A dozen thoughts jumbled together. A portal was a door. It opened and closed the way a door did. What if it didn't disappear in between those openings and closings? What if it remained unseen, waiting for—oh, I don't know—a vortex to pull in the power needed to open it?

Leaping to my feet, I bellowed at Harry to fly faster, because fucking hell, it was worth a try. I seized Lucan's wrists and began dragging him up the remaining hill to the stone. I didn't know if he was alive or if he would survive the trip home or if we would even make it home, but I couldn't leave him here. Not alone.

My gaze fell on Morgana, and I hesitated. *Oh, my goddess, but to reunite her with Keven ...*

Harry's vortex tugged at my shirt and the hill rumbled beneath my feet. I looked up at the forest, half gone now, and then back at Morgana as Lucan's weight dragged at my arms. The grief of having to choose flooded my eyes with more tears. I would never manage to get both of them into the vortex. Not in time.

Harry called out as he circled overhead, and the plaintiveness in the cry stabbed through me. I threw a glance over my shoulder to gauge distance, then dropped Lucan's hands and bolted across and down the hill. Because I might not be able to manage two adult bodies, but I could absolutely manage a cat who deserved to at least be buried at home.

The hill shook harder as I stumbled to a halt and snatched up the limp body of my Gus. I tucked the cat inside my sweater, tucked the bottom of my sweater into my jeans waistband to hold him there, and staggered back up the now-heaving hill to collect Lucan.

But the goliath I'd thought dead had beaten me to it. He crawled toward the stone, dragging Lucan behind him. The shifter's hair and clothing flapped wildly in the wind as they neared, and then the goliath half lifted, half pushed Lucan through the vortex wall. The shifter landed in the middle—in the eye—and the flapping stopped.

Lying on its side, the goliath watched through its remaining eye as I approached it, rumbling its anxiety and disapproval as it tried to motion me toward the vortex instead.

I knelt at its side because it deserved no less from me. "Thank you, my liege," I said simply. I pressed my lips to the broken hand, and then, as the forest at the base of the hill crumbled away, I stood and threw myself through the wall of the vortex after Lucan.

Harry's wings alone weren't enough, so I did what I'd seen Morok do in New York. I threw my arms wide and began spinning as fast as I could.

Remarkably, thankfully, I felt no vertigo. In fact, the faster I spun, the clearer the world around me seemed to get. The wall of wind became the individual particles it carried, each seemingly suspended without moving. Beyond it, Camlann dissolved in slow motion—disappearing a frame at a time as my gaze swept over it on each pass. Above the vortex, a seething mass of clouds gathered inside a perimeter of dark flames, growing denser, more opaque.

And inside it, the power—

My spinning faltered. Where was the power? It should be forming. Should be building. But it wasn't. I cast my mind back to New York again, to what had been the final catalyst— and then I remembered. Remembered how I had rooted myself in the Earth and called on Fire and Water and Air and etched sigils into a sphere of every color that had ever existed and—

Despair tugged at me again. Morgana's body had disappeared from the hill now, and the Between was almost here. I had no time for sigils, and not enough Earth in which to root myself. Not enough Water or Air or—

Outside the vortex, the sphere that held Morok flew toward the wall as the wind sucked it in, closer each time my helpless gaze landed on it. Closer. Closer. Dear goddess, even if I did manage to open the portal now, the damned thing would go through with us, and what if the god inside still lived? What—

The world outside the vortex slowed further, and in the same slow motion with which the hill below it dissolved, a granite hand lifted to snatch the sphere out of the air. Hand, sphere, and the remainder of Camlann dissolved into the Between.

Except for us. Except for the stone.

The stone.

I slammed one foot into the ground, stopping my spin with a jolt that felt like it dislocated every vertebra in my spine. .

The stone.

I whirled toward the last piece of the Camlann splinter and placed a hand on each of its broken pieces. Of all the things to have come out of Camelot or the legend of King Arthur, the stone was one of the most enduring. Trees died and fell and fed new growth. Cities and castles disappeared beneath new layers. People died.

But stones? Stones endured.

Stones were ageless.

Stones *were* Earth.

Especially magickal ones.

I lifted my hands from the stone that had become one again, drawing the roots of Earth itself from the healed pieces. Power surged between my palms. I cradled it, breathed into it, joined with it—and slowly wrapped it into the magick of opening. The magick that was solid and ephemeral at the same time. Magick that was all the colors that had ever existed and none of them at all. Magick that was translucent and opaque and dark and light and …

Me. The magick was me. And once again, it was ready.

I lifted the orb I'd created high, took one last breath, and tossed it into the center of the unopened portal above us. At the last instant, as I turned away from the brilliant flash of light, I seized Harry's tail and pulled him from the vortex wall, down to our one remaining, precious piece of ground. Then, with my cat warm against my skin inside my sweater, and my shifter and dragon at my feet, I reached for the open portal.

"There's no place like home," I whispered to it as the last bit of Camlann vanished in a puff of dust.

Wait … my cat was warm?

ALSO BY

The Crone Wars

Becoming Crone

A Gathering of Crones

Game of Crones

Crone Unleashed

Rise of the Crones (Spring 2024)

The Grigori Legacy

Sins of the Angels (Grigori Legacy book 1)

Sins of the Son (Grigori Legacy book 2)

Sins of the Lost (Grigori Legacy book 3)

Sins of the Warrior (Grigori Legacy book 4)

Other Books by Linda Poitevin

The Ever After Romance Collection

Gwynneth Ever After

Forever After

Forever Grace

Always and Forever

Abigail Always

Shadow of Doubt

ACKNOWLEDGEMENTS

I'm always a little surprised when I finish a book and think, "Well, look at that. I did it!" But the truth is, it's not just about me because I never do it alone.

So here's a great big squishy thank you to all the amazing people who have helped me bring Claire to life: my friend and copy editor extraordinaire, Laura Paquet; my life coach and friend, Diana Hynes; my amazing cover designer, Deranged Doctor Design; my interior layout designer, Priya; and beta readers Lana Yakimchuk, Pam Samson, Lena Smith, and Tess Reardon. I couldn't have done this without any of you, and I'm so very thankful to have you behind me.

A special shout-out goes to the bestest writing buddy in the world, Marie Bilodeau, whose ability to listen to me whine about the story (when I should just be writing the story!) is mind-boggling. Thank you for your patience, support, and love, Marie. I can't imagine my life without you in it.

And then, of course, there's my husband. Pat, you have been my rock, my anchor, and my greatest inspiration in life. Your unwavering belief in me has held me up when my own belief wavered, and I cannot begin to tell you how grateful I am to share my life with you. I love you.

Last but not least, a thank you to you, dear reader, because Claire may have been born of my imagination, but she lives because of you. I'm so very glad you love her as much as I do.

About The Author

Lydia M. Hawke is a pseudonym used by me, Linda Poitevin, for my urban fantasy books. Together, we are the author of books that range from supernatural suspense thrillers to contemporary romances and romantic suspense.

Originally from beautiful British Columbia, I moved to Canada's capital region of Ottawa-Gatineau more than thirty years ago with the love of my life. Which means I've been married most of my life now, and I've spent most of it here. Wow. Anyway, when I'm not plotting the world's downfall or next great love story, I'm also a wife, mom, grandma, friend, walker of a Giant Dog, keeper of many cats, and an avid gardener and food preserver. My next great ambition in life (other than writing the next book, of course) is to have an urban chicken coop. Yes, seriously…because chickens.

You can find me hanging out on Facebook at facebook.com/LydiaMHawke, and on my website at LydiaHawkeBooks.com, where you can also join my newsletter for updates on new books (and a free story!)

I love to hear from readers and can be reached at lydia@lydiahawkebooks.com. And yes, I answer all my emails!